Space Drifters:
The Iron Gauntlet

BOOK TWO

Paul Regnier

an imprint of
GILEAD PUBLISHING

The Iron Gauntlet by Paul Regnier
Published by Enclave Publishing,
an imprint of Gilead Publishing,
Wheaton, IL 60187
www.enclavepublishing.com

ISBN: 978-1-68370-008-1

Space Drifters: The Iron Gauntlet
© 2016 by Paul Regnier

Published in the United States by Enclave Publishing, an imprint of Gilead Publishing Wheaton, Illinois.

Cover designed by Kirk DouPonce
Edited by Andy Meisenheimer
Interior designed by Beth Shagene

Printed in the United States of America

For Joshua and Katie,
the bright stars in my night sky.

CHAPTER 1

ANOTHER REASON TO HATE GLOWING ORBS

ALTHOUGH I'D JUST SET FOOT on the blue sands of the alien planet, I knew the ambush was coming. The somber grey sky added an extra layer of creepy to the barren waste. The moon slithered between the procession of dark clouds, casting uneven patches of light across the terrain.

The air was dry and smelled of ash. Low hills spread out before me covered with the white stones of an old, ruined civilization, collapsed pillars leaning like weary guardians planted long ago in the ancient sand. In the distance an ivory temple with a domed roof rose above the landscape. A soft glow came from within, which made it a safe bet that the sphere I was after was inside.

All I had to do was get there without dying.

I drew the thin, black laser pistol holstered at my side and powered it to full. It emitted a high-pitched noise, like a kitten trapped in a well. Finally a soft bell went off as a little green light on the barrel lit up to indicate it was ready to fire. I looked down at the small gun and sighed. I was thoroughly embarrassed to be holding such a feeble weapon.

Something shuffled across the sand nearby.

I crept behind a collapsed archway and flattened against the chalky surface. In the clearing before me were several fallen pillars leaning against a crumbling stone table. A small figure huddled in the shadows. I froze, taking shallow breaths to remain noiseless.

The dark, olive green head of a moon goblin peeked out from the table. His beady black eyes took in the clearing in a series of twitchy glances, and then he dashed into the open, heading for a nearby pillar. I spun clear of the archway, the barrel of my pistol moving in sync with the fleeing creature. A squeeze of the trigger and two sprite-like blasts of green energy rocketed into the goblin. He ignited and fell headlong into the fine sand. A soft cloud of blue dust hovered around his fallen form. Within moments, all that remained was a skeleton lying motionless on the planet's surface.

I grinned and lifted the gun to my chin, blowing at the smoking barrel. "Take that."

"Hey," the fallen goblin skeleton sat up, facing me. His skull was of course expressionless, so I could only guess what he was thinking. He pointed a skeletal finger at me. "You said it wouldn't hurt."

"No." I waved my pistol like the correcting finger of a parent. "I said it wouldn't hurt *much*. I just mumbled the much part so you wouldn't hear."

The goblin skeleton stood and rubbed its skull. "Well, that's deceptive, which is just as bad as lying."

"Yes, only much trickier," I said. "Stick around. You might learn something from me."

"Learn from *this*," a voice called out behind me.

I turned just in time to see a dark-blue pantherwoman

leaping toward me, hind paws first. The thick paws thudded against my chest and launched me backward. A rough landing on the sand knocked the wind out of me.

I rolled to my side, struggling to catch my breath, the ashen air burning my lungs as I gasped. The pantherwoman had vanished, and my pistol was half buried in the sand a few feet away. My hands and knees kicked up blue dust as I scrambled toward it. A freem before it was in my grasp, the dark paws of the pantherwoman landed on it. The frail pistol broke into black shards. A dim green light flashed under the paws for a moment before fading away.

"My, my." The pantherwoman retrieved a heavy laser rifle from her back and trained it on my head. "Alone and unarmed in the cobalt sands. That stings."

"Not as much as this." I grabbed the last concussion pellet from my belt and threw it toward her. It exploded near her head in a white cloud of smoke. She let out a small scream as I rolled to my feet and sprinted away.

I threaded a quick path through the crumbling structures, looking toward the horizon. It wasn't long until my goal lay before me—a large, whitewashed temple. A brief sprint brought me under the shadow of the thick pillars that encircled the open-air temple, supporting the dome-shaped roof. It sat high above the surrounding landscape at the peak of a stone stairway. A bright yellow glow shone from within.

I raced up the stairs, checking behind now and again for pursuers. At the top of the stairs, I saw the object of my quest—a golden sphere resting on a pedestal. It bathed the area in its radiant light.

The temple was most likely riddled with traps, but I had no time to play it cautious. I crept forward on the balls of my feet, ready to dive away at the first sound of a trap being triggered. Near the pedestal the golden light was blinding. A soft twinkling of bells rang in my ears, and pleasant waves of heat emanated from the sphere that lay within arm's reach.

It was all too easy.

I took a deep breath and steadied myself. In one fluid motion I grabbed the sphere and rolled away to avoid the inevitable falling cage or collapsing floor. As I rolled to a stop, the golden light went dim. The planet's cold blue light crept in, and I suddenly felt like I was in a tomb.

An eerie sound came from the ceiling overhead, as if a torrent of hail was falling. Within a few sickening moments, dozens of space monkeys scrambled into view, their hideous forms pouring down the surrounding pillars. They came from all sides and at such frightening speed I knew I'd be trapped. Their piercing screeches filled the air and echoed against the marble floor. I leapt to my feet in pure terror, the sight of space monkeys churning my stomach. Mangy, orange fur ... grasping claws ... never-blinking bloodshot eyes.

The sphere in my hands went dark as if to confirm my doom, and a deep bellow came from outside the temple. There was a sharp, screeching commotion from the monkey ranks and they scampered away, clearing a wide path.

The broad shadow of an approaching creature fell over them, and in the blue moonlight I saw a nasty looking beast. He stepped into the temple, a disturbing combination of gorilla and rhino, tufts of black fur intermingling with his thick, grey hide.

The creature flashed poisonous green eyes at me, and a broad, fang-toothed grin spread across its mouth. "O foolish man of dark designs. You have availed naught but a farce." He raised his hands in a theatrical flourish. "The false light of your darkened path has led you to ruin. Now behold your calamity and indulge in lamentations." It broke into a victorious, mocking laugh.

I hesitated for a moment. "Um ... what?"

The beast put its hands on its hips and let out an agitated growl. "Your calamity." It motioned to the surrounding monkeys. "The chosen farce." He pointed at the dim sphere in my hands. He nodded as if waiting for me to understand something simple.

I shrugged. Were the nearby translators working?

The beast sighed, looking defeated. "It's a decoy sphere. You chose the wrong one and now you're surrounded and you lose. Got it?"

"Oh." I nodded. "So, you're saying I've lost."

He motioned to the monkeys again. "I believe that's apparent."

I stepped toward him. "But ... what if I already found the real sphere, then switched it with your decoy just to add personal insult to your defeat?"

The beast folded his arms and huffed a laugh. "Preposterous. The only way to—"

He was cut short as I chucked the sphere at his head. He threw up his hands to block it as I sprinted past.

The broad path between the monkey ranks still remained, so I bolted right through it. The monkeys screeched in fury and closed ranks, their clawed fingers reaching for me. Two of them leapt into my path, blocking the escape. I threw caution to the wind and dove toward them, but the mangy fur of their disgusting, gangly bodies covered me. I retched, struggling to keep down breakfast. The impact sent us all tumbling down the stairs in a painful tangle of fur and skin.

There were several freems of jolting collisions and monkey screeching before I reached the base of the stairs. The soft sand of the planet's surface brought me to a stop. As I looked up into the night sky, I heard a few creatures approaching. Spinning into a threatening fighting stance was my first thought, but my body had other plans. After the nasty spill down the stairs, all I could do was lie there, gasping for air.

The hulking gorilla beast loomed over me. "Clumsy and predictable." He gave a patronizing shake of his head. "Not to mention ineffective."

The pantherwoman walked up on the opposite side. She looked down at me and sighed. "Well, he lasted a bit longer this time."

The moon goblin skeleton joined her. He cocked his skull to the side as if confused by my condition. "He doesn't look so good. Maybe we should take a break."

"Quite right, Nelvan." The gorilla beast looked skyward and raised his voice. "End training simulation."

The sky dissolved, and the black paneled, vaulted ceiling of a virtual training room took its place. We'd landed at Quingrilloc space station this morning; it was known for its sim training rooms. It was also known for its taxidermy, the passageways from room to room being lined with the preserved forms of alien creatures frozen in hideous states of aggression.

Quingrilloc was our last stop on the way to the superplanet Fantasmica, home of the Iron Gauntlet challenge, and my last opportunity to prepare for the dangerous games I'd been selected to compete in.

The goblin skeleton faded away, replaced by a worried-looking Nelvan. He reached down to me. "Captain, you okay?"

I waved a hand dismissively. "Course I'm okay." I stood too quickly, attempting to prove my strength. My head started spinning, and I stumbled.

The pantherwoman rushed to my side. "Glint, I think Nelvan's right. You should rest a bit." The pantherwoman illusion dissolved and there was Jasette, looking as beautiful as ever. Her blue and silver streaked hair was done up in a tight braid, draped across her shoulder like she'd tamed some exotic snake.

"Captain, this is not good." The gorilla beast faded away and there stood Blix, my copper-scaled first mate. He was still shaking his head at me. "The competitor reception is tonight and the first challenge starts tomorrow. You're nowhere near ready."

"Maybe this isn't such a good idea." Subtle lines of concern filled Nelvan's face. "I've been hearing brutal stuff about this Iron Gauntlet competition on the uniweb. The captain could really get hurt."

"I'm fine," I lied. "I got this." I snapped my black kandrelian-hide jacket taut to emphasize my confidence. Truth be told, my body was exhausted. We'd only gone through two training simulations, but since my exercise regimen is spotty and my food choices are generally covered in a thick, greasy batter, my stamina wasn't optimal.

Blix narrowed his reptilian gaze at me and grinned. "Then perhaps we should raise it up to level five, eh, Captain?" He rubbed his hands together like an excited child.

Simulated or not, it was all too real once the illusion

started. Even though the permanent damage limiters were activated, the bumps and bruises were enough to make my insides all twitchy.

Still, I couldn't look weak in front of my crew. I gave him a look of determination. "Bring it on, lizard boy."

Blix's lips parted, revealing twin rows of sharp teeth. He gave a low hiss. "Indeed I will." He signaled to the others. "Places everyone. Instructions and armaments will be waiting for you."

"Wait, Blix." Jasette looked at me, her face tense. "I think we should take that break."

Blix turned to Jasette with a hostile glare. She shook her head. He exhaled deeply and slouched down. "Oh, very well. We'll take a ten jemmin break."

"Um," Nelvan furrowed his brow. "I forget. A jemmin is an earth minute, right?"

"Very similar." Blix said.

"Nelvan, you've gotta lose those old earth terms," I said. "Zorwellian Gate time is a superior calendar. Forget about seconds, minutes, and hours, it's freems, jemmins, and trids. And no more months or years, it's montuls and gloons. Got it?"

Nelvan gave an unconvincing nod. "I think so."

The wide, steel door to the control room slid open and a technician in a grey jumpsuit peered in. "If you're all done in here, we need to cycle the sim emitters."

Blix motioned to him. "Yes, we'll take a short break."

The technician nodded. "Okay, the snack room is open."

"Ah, snacks." A broad smile covered Blix's face. "Just what we need to prepare for the next training."

"Yeah." Nelvan held his stomach. "I'm really hungry. It's not that weird frozen worm thing again, right?"

"Blerk tendrils," Blix corrected. "Unfortunately, no. The fare here is far more pedestrian. Mostly fried meats and crispy foods."

Nelvan let out a sigh of relief.

"You two go ahead," Jasette said. "We'll catch up."

Blix led Nelvan from the room and Jasette turned to me. She took a deep breath, which of course meant trouble. She'd obviously spent time thinking over something I was unaware of and had come to a conclusion.

Jasette paused, her eyes locked onto mine. "You don't have to do this. There's still time to back out of the competition."

Her words caught me off guard. Instead of my relationship inadequacies, she was talking about the deadly Iron Gauntlet, which for some reason at the moment seemed less frightening than navigating an adult relationship. Even though it was dangerous, I had already resigned myself to the competition. It was a quick path to getting the kind of money necessary to change my situation. Winning the Iron Gauntlet and nabbing a million vibes meant a better ship, high-end equipment, and a shot at upscale clientele that actually paid well for missions. My current pool of thug employers had a bad habit of trying to kill you to get out of paying for completed assignments. Too many gloons scraping by as a star pilot for hire and living on bare essentials was enough to drive a person insane—I had reached my fill of the meager life and was ready to risk it all to turn my life around.

I had to reassure her that the competition was my best shot. "Why would I back out? There's a million vibes out there with my name on them."

"Or a tombstone," she said.

I tapped at the Emerald Enigma, the gemstone hanging from my neck. "I've got this. I'll be fine."

"That thing is dangerous." She pointed at my chest. "Remember Grizzolo? You want to end up a cautionary tale too?"

She had a good point. The thought of turning into a spider-legged, corpse-skinned freak was definitely not part of my plan. But this was a chance of a lifetime. How could I let it slip by?

"I'm tired of struggling just to survive," I said.

"I understand Glint, but you can't be so reckless."

A painful memory hit, and before I could stop myself it spilled out. "I guess I should play it safe like my parents did. Slaving away every day in 'safe' jobs, earning enough for a meager living. Until an alien virus sweeps through our city and takes out half the population. It sure worked out well for them, didn't it?" Her face tightened. I paused, wishing I could take back my words. "I'm sorry. Look, my head's a mess right now." I made it a habit not to bring up painful memories from childhood. It was like putting a dagger in an old wound. Somehow in the emotional rush of the impending challenge and my growing connection with Jasette, that pain jumped to the surface. I had to stuff it down and convince her that I knew what I was doing.

I moved closer and fixed her with a confident gaze. "Look, all I know is: life's a gamble no matter which path you take. You might as well make it a good gamble, right?"

"I'm sorry about your parents. I had no idea."

I nodded. "Yeah, me too."

She grabbed my hand. "I never said to play it safe, just don't play it crazy, okay?"

I shook my head. "It's not crazy, the Enigma will—"

Jasette put a finger over my lips, stopping my words. "Just promise me you'll think about what I said, okay?"

"Okay."

She gave me a quick kiss, then drew back, studying my face. "You ready to join the others?"

I needed a moment to gather my thoughts. "Not yet."

Jasette nodded. "Take your time."

Soon she was out of the room and I was left alone with my cloudy thoughts. Maybe she was right. A million vibes was the prize of a lifetime, but what exactly was I getting myself into? I rubbed a sore spot on my arm. My adrenaline rush from the training was long gone. Fresh pains sprang up around my body like nagging reminders of all the mistakes I'd made. It was time for a well-earned rest in the med unit. The pain seemed to echo Jasette's warning. Was the risk worth it? Maybe it was time to cut my losses and exit the Iron Gauntlet before something happened that the med unit couldn't fix.

I'd turned for the exit door when all the lights went out.

"Hey!" I called out. "I'm still in here."

I waited for a few moments in the darkness but received no response. I was about to grope my way to the exit when I heard something move. I froze. A low noise vibrated in my ears, followed by a cylindrical beam of light shooting upward. The column of light shone a few feet in front of me, illuminating a slender figure hidden in the shadows of a dark cloak.

"Stop the simulator," I called out. "I'm taking a break."

"This is no simulation." The hooded figure spoke in a raspy, hissing voice.

A series of cylindrical lights shot up around the room, showcasing a host of dark, wraith-like creatures, as if shadows had torn free from the corners of the room by some dark magic. The tattered edges of their black forms hung suspended above the lights, hovering in a slow, hypnotic rhythm. They had no faces or expressions by which to judge them, but I had a strong impression they intended to do horrible things.

My adrenaline shot up again. I instinctively grabbed for my DEMOTER, only to be greeted by an empty holster. Without a weapon I was vulnerable. My thoughts rushed to the fifty-thousand vibe bounty on my head.

I widened my stance and put a hand behind my back like I had a hidden weapon. "What do you want?" I threw as much low growl into my voice as possible.

The figure spread its arms wide, revealing silver, scaled hands covered in short quills. "You, of course."

CHAPTER 2

THE PARALLAX WAGER

MY SITUATION LOOKED GRIM and the games hadn't even started yet. There was no telling what powers this hooded figure and his wraith minions held, but it was clear I was outmatched. My only chance was to bluff my way out of it.

"You came to collect my bounty, huh?" I narrowed my eyes and tried to sound dangerous. "My crew is waiting outside, and my first mate is a Vythian who shows no mercy. I'd leave now before anything messy happens to you."

An amused laugh hissed out of the hood. "They are fully engaged in the snack room. We are keeping watch over their every move."

I swallowed hard. "Unless your minions were already dispatched by my crew." It was a desperate bluff but it was all I had.

The figure sighed. "Captain Starcrost, your empty threats are pointless." The voice of the creature sounded like pressure escaping an air lock. "Besides, I haven't come for your bounty." The creature pulled back the hood revealing a silver, snake-like head. Thin rows of quills trailed from the luminous blue eyes down its neck. "I've come to *help* you."

I was speechless for several freems as my mind tried to recalibrate. "Help me how?"

"My name is Silvet. I am a messenger." The creature's silver hands folded neatly in front of it. "My master offers you help to win the Iron Gauntlet."

To have a shady messenger deliver an offer of help was a nice change of pace. Far better than the usual threats of being frozen for cheating at cards, thrown into a slug pit for flirting with the master's daughter, tied to the back of a slarn in heat for delivering the wrong shipment, and so on. With the typical dark warnings out of the picture, I relaxed a bit.

"Who's your master," I said, "and why should he help me?"

"My master holds anonymity sacred. But to prove the validity of the offer, know that you have found favor with the great Parallax."

My mind rushed through the long list of thugs in the universe and came up empty. "Never heard of him."

"Nor would you. Parallax dwells in the shadows of the galaxy, pulling the unseen strings of power and altering the course of events."

I gave an unsure nod. "Okay.... So what does he want from me?"

Silvet lowered its snaky head. "Your odds of winning the Gauntlet have been calculated as the lowest of any player in fifty seasons of the game. All the smart money is against you."

I frowned. "*This* is how you're gonna help me?"

The creature gave a graceful wave of its hand. "Allow me

to finish. Parallax is betting on you to win. The payout for a wager on such a longshot would increase my master's power in the universe by tenfold."

A lump formed in my throat. My thoughts of backing out of the competition crumbled away. "What if I decide not to compete?"

Silvet's eyes narrowed. "That would be unwise."

The picture became clear. I was the pawn in some big-time gambler's wager. But there was one thing the rough and tumble galaxy had taught me. Even if you're a pawn, you're still playing the game. And this was my chance to make the most of my game.

I folded my arms in front of my chest and wore a detached expression, like I wasn't impressed with this powerful boss and the creepy wraith minions. "So what kind of help is Parallax offering?"

"Whatever you feel is necessary to improve your chances."

I liked where the conversation was heading. "I need a new DEMOTER. Don't suppose you have one of those handy?"

Silvet gave a subtle shake of its head. "My powers have no need of supplemental weapons. But rest assured, I can obtain one."

"Make it a Y-series. They pack the biggest punch."

"Captain Starcrost, the means at my disposal can secure the weapon of your choice. There's no need to limit yourself to old technology."

The vein in my neck throbbed with anger at the insult to the finest energy blaster ever created. "Newer doesn't mean better. The DEMOTER is what I want."

"So be it. In the meantime ..." Silvet took a few steps forward, the luminous column of light following. "Accept this offer of good faith on behalf of Parallax." The creature produced a black pouch from its cloak and opened it wide. The warm, green glow of vibes shone out.

My mouth hung open. These weren't common street vibes—these were nothing less than high-class vibe spheres. A far purer form of vibe energy and—more importantly— value. Green light danced inside the vibe spheres like trapped fireflies. My eyes darted across the bright currency making a quick tally.

"There's gotta be ten thousand worth of vibes in there." I said.

A subtle grin spread across its serpentine features. "And there's more where that came from."

The sweet glow of prosperity held my eyes like a tractor beam. It was difficult to think straight. I suddenly became aware that drool was pooling around my lower lip.

I tore my attention away from the money. "What's the catch?"

"It's quite simple. Win the game."

"And what happens if I don't win?"

The creature arched its brow. "Haven't you watched The Iron Gauntlet?"

I nodded. The negative effects of losing would be received from the deadly competition itself.

Silvet lifted the pouch of vibes toward me. "So, do we have a deal, Captain?"

It was almost never a good idea to get involved with shadowy power players of the universe, but if this Parallax character had already bet on me, backing out of the competition would probably be a death sentence. Not to mention I already had a large bounty placed on my head by Mar Mar the Unthinkable, the biggest thug lord in the galaxy. I had no way of paying off that bounty aside from winning the competition. When I considered the alternatives, it almost seemed crazy not to accept.

I took the black pouch and gave a wry grin. "Deal."

Silvet smiled, its forked tongue briefly flicking out. "Excellent. Parallax will be pleased." The creature turned and walked a few steps away, then spun back around. "Oh, and Captain?"

"Yeah?"

"You must not mention this deal or the name of Parallax to anyone."

I swallowed hard. "Anyone?"

The silver color of its skin seemed to drain away, replaced by a pinkish hue. Wavy, unkempt blonde hair grew out of its scalp. I gasped as Silvet turned into an exact replica of Nelvan. "Make sure you don't tell me." Nelvan's signature teen voice squeaked. The figure morphed again, growing larger and covered with copper scales. Within a few brief moments it had transformed into Blix. "Don't tell me either, Captain." Another strange metamorphosis took place until it resembled Jasette. "Or especially me."

I was definitely in trouble. Changelings were rare in the universe. Because of their unique abilities, they were generally mistrusted and often mistreated. Most changelings chose a favorite form and stuck with it, seeking a normal way of life. The ones that embraced their ability had to become skilled enough to evade or overcome those who came against them. As a result, they were some of the more dangerous beings to find yourself at odds with. If Silvet was just a messenger, it spoke volumes of the power of its master, Parallax.

The Jasette figure motioned to the floating wraith creatures. In a blur of motion, they huddled around her. She beheld me with her familiar green eyes. They had never looked so deadly. "My minions will be watching. Do as I say and you will find yourself a very rich man, Captain Starcrost."

The Jasette clone drew the cloak over her head and the lights in the room went out.

CHAPTER 3

BRUISES AND
BODYSUITS

MY LIFE WAS A MAGNET for bad news. I was a dead man if I avoided this deal, but if I went along with it, there was a good chance of dying in the Iron Gauntlet. At least the competition left a chance of victory, slim as it was. I only wished I could tell my crew, especially Jasette. How could I convince her that backing out was not an option?

I'd tucked the vibe spheres away in my chambers, and was laid out in the med unit of my ship. I needed to wait for a time when I could bring them out without raising a host of questions from my crew.

The heated gel cushion of the patient slab in the med unit was acting up again. My back felt like it was burning while my legs prickled with goose bumps. Just a few days ago I would have complained, but after I returned the Glekthork refugees to their planet, there was no one left to tackle the intricate star freighter repairs. Only a day after their departure I'd flown too close to a meteor storm, and in a few moments of jarring collisions, all the restorative work of the

Glekthork engineers had been undone and once again my ship was in need of repairs.

I sat up to alleviate the burning and swung my legs off the cold side of the slab. Blix had talked me into wearing his specially designed golden "med shorts." He claimed they aided the healing process but I had my suspicions he was just trying to make me look stupid and laugh about it secretly. I grabbed my classic black space captain pants from the hook nearby and exchanged them for the glittery shorts. I reached for my lucky silver shirt and froze, hearing someone approaching. My mind pictured Silvet's wraith minions lurking through the dark corners of the ship. A shiver went through me at the thought.

Blix walked into the med lab and a wave of relief washed over me. He was tapping out commands on his translucent com screen as he approached.

He looked up and gave a scolding shake of his head. "Captain, what are you doing? You need to lie down so your frail human body can heal properly."

Blix collapsed the com screen to palm size and attached it to his belt. He moved closer and started checking the med patches spread generously over my bare torso. Their digital readouts glowed and beeped upon his touch, bragging about how much faster they were working than my natural healing processes.

"There, you see? Only seventy two percent." He paused for a moment, his expression softening. "Captain, I must confess, I'm having misgivings about this competition. Are you quite sure you wish to go through with this?"

Blix seemed genuinely concerned. At that moment I fought the desire to tell him about Silvet and the deal I'd made. After all we'd been through in the last few gloons I felt that I owed it to him. But I couldn't forget Silvet's warning. The last thing I wanted to do was put Blix in danger.

"Don't worry, I'll be fine," I lied. "I have to do this. The Enigma will protect me."

He gave a slow nod. "As you wish, Captain. But if we're going to do this, we need to do it properly. Soon we'll be in the midst of high society and we need to look the part. We arrive in Fantasmica in a little under a trid and I haven't even chosen a proper outfit for the reception because I have to keep babysitting you."

I gave him a dark look. "Hey, I'm about to enter a lethal challenge tomorrow and you're worrying about what to wear?"

"Captain, this is no ordinary reception. We'll be in the presence of the most influential beings in the universe."

I scowled and grabbed my shirt, throwing it on over the med patches. "Who cares about some stuffy celebs. I suffered through *ten* of your insane training exercises today. How 'bout a little concern?"

"That's preposterous, I'm filled with concern." Blix crossed his arms and lifted his chin as if offended. "I'm concerned with your poor performance today."

That was all I could take. All my peacemaking molecules scurried away and prepared for the inevitable rage response. My fist decided it had had enough, and so I took a broad swing at his meaty, reptilian head. He ducked and spun away easily. I fell to my hands and knees with the effort.

Blix gave a scolding click of his tongue. "Captain, really now. Such barbarics are beneath your position."

I looked up with a scowl. "A good punch in the face is never beneath me."

He laughed. "You call that a good punch?"

In an instant I was back on my feet, poised in my best fighting stance. "Alright, you asked for it."

I took another swing. Eventually, I thought, the power of the Emerald Enigma hanging around my neck would kick in. My fist hit nothing but air as I lunged forward and Blix weaved to the side.

He shook his head. "I do wish you would control yourself."

A sneaky thought hit me. "Hey, what happened to your new Christian vows?" I pointed an accusing finger at him. "Aren't you supposed to turn the other cheek?"

"Yes Captain, but if you can't hit my cheek in the first place, how am I to turn the other?" He grinned, his sharp teeth mocking me like an army of miniature pikemen.

There was an empty metal food tray lying on the vitals monitor nearby. I lifted it over my shoulder, preparing for the next strike. "We'll see about that."

My attack was cut short when Jasette walked through the door. She paused, giving us a confused look. "What's going on?"

Blix assumed a dignified stance. "The captain is being quite irrational."

Jasette glanced at the raised food tray, then back at me. "You're attacking your first mate?"

I lowered the tray and pointed at him. "He started it."

Jasette raised a hand toward each of us. "We're coming up on Fantasmica soon. You two need to get dressed."

Blix cast a repulsed look at my clothes. "Indeed." He

turned and walked out the door, his head lifted in a look of superiority.

Jasette shook her head at me. "Should I be worried about your immature behavior at the reception?"

I put the tray back on the vitals monitor. "Don't worry, I know how to fake it with all those high brows."

She paused. "We'll be there soon. Have you thought about what I said?"

As badly as I wanted to tell her about Parallax and the deal, once again I was stuck between honesty and putting my crew in danger. For all I knew, those shadow minions were aboard my ship listening to every word I said.

"Look, I know what I'm doing seems stupid," I said.

"*Seems* stupid?"

"Okay, there's a degree of crazy involved, but you have to trust me."

She leaned back and folded her arms. "Okay, if that's your decision, then …" Her expression went from concern to detached. "Forget it. Let's go. We have to get ready for the reception."

Jasette turned and led the way out of the med lab. We headed down the hallway toward our quarters. The brushed steel walls were trumpeting their grey, steel machismo in the glow of the overhead lighting. Jasette walked next to me, looking straight ahead and keeping way too quiet. Something was obviously on her mind. I wasn't always the best at picking up subtle female hints, but this was unmistakable. Her head was most likely awhirl with thoughts and emotions. I had to tread carefully. I figured a compliment would break the silence nicely.

"You look good today," I said.

Jasette frowned and gave me a sidelong glare. "You saying I haven't been looking good lately?"

"What? No, you're always beautiful." I tried a jovial tone hoping to shoo away the tension. "Plus, your power suit compliments your shape."

"My shape?" She stopped and turned on me. "Like I'm parading around for you to check me out all day?"

"Hey, it's your suit. Obviously you want me to look."

As soon as the words were out of my mouth I realized all was lost.

Her eyes went all squinty and dangerous. "For your information perv, the contours of this suit are specially designed for enhanced physical performance. I didn't pick it so you could leer at me."

"But you like when I notice, right?"

She let out an exasperated grunt. "I had something important to tell you." She started jabbing her finger toward my chest. She was probably fantasizing it was a knife. "Now I can't even look at you." She stormed down the hall.

"Hey, Jasette." I tried to use the calm tone that communicates she's totally overreacting. "Come on, I—"

"Save it." She held up a hand without looking back and continued down the hall.

Once again I was disappointed in the Enigma for not stepping in with some good luck. Obviously the rhyme and reason behind its operations were still beyond my grasp. I sighed and headed for my chambers. If I had to go to some snooty celebrity reception, I might as well grab my jacket.

CHAPTER 4

FANTASMICA FASHION

A HIGH, SINGLE TONE sounded in my quarters.

"Approaching the superplanet Fantasmica," Iris said. "The crew is waiting for you on the bridge, Captain."

"Got it." I tightened the belt around my waist and cast a mournful look at the empty holster resting against my thigh.

Ever since my trusty DEMOTER gave its life by exploding and sending my old nemesis Hamilton Von Drone and his creepy robot into a river of lava, I was weaponless. It was an empty, cold feeling. I was a nebula serpent without its fangs, a toxic moon slug without its secretions, a zeluvian omni vortex without its refracting, ethereal, quadrant reverters. And so on.

There were various blasters for sale at the Quingrilloc training space station, but they were all too wimpy for my taste. The new trend was slimline pistols with those careful, surgical types of strikes. Boring. I missed the raw, unwieldy power of the DEMOTER that left impact blasts not soon forgotten.

Blix said it was a clumsy, dangerous weapon but he

25

completely missed the intimidation factor. Refined space explorers more accustomed to delicate guns would cringe at the sight of it. Plus, it sounded like a beast when it fired. Call me old fashioned but I prefer a weapon that packs a punch, wild or not.

"Computer, enable reflection pane," I said.

"Yes, Captain."

The wall before me dissolved into a mirror. I had to admit, my appearance was a little slouchy and tired. I stood up straight, smoothed the wrinkles from my lucky silver shirt and adjusted my jacket. It helped a little. I narrowed my gaze and tightened my jaw like the confident, determined starship captain persona I wanted to project.

"That's nice, Captain," Iris said. "I'd remember that look if I were you."

I frowned at the ceiling. "Computer, do you mind? I'd like some privacy once in a while."

"Of course, Captain. I'll look away."

I was pretty sure she was bluffing. It was always a pain point for me that a starship captain retains no real privacy. Once you're on board with a supercomputer that never sleeps, the ever-watchful digital eye was a difficult thing to get used to.

The intercom buzzed to life. "Captain, are you nearly ready?" Blix said. "We're all waiting on you."

"I know, I know, I'll be there soon." I ran my hands through my hair, trying to get more of the symmetrical, feathered look typical of space captains in all the flashy advertisements, but my coarse dark hair wasn't playing nice. It always looked more like I just woke from a nap. There were a few women that seemed to go for that ruffian look but generally those were the hardened, space bar types. There was little chance it would win anyone over at the pompous reception.

I sighed, resigning myself to an uncouth destiny and headed out of my quarters.

Moments later the lift doors chirped open and I entered the bridge. My crew were already there, watching me with questioning eyes.

"Captain, we're landing in a few jemmins." Blix made an exasperated motion to the viewing screen. We were descending through the puffy clouds of planet Fantasmica. Breaks in the cloud cover revealed green landscapes and golden oceans below. "Why aren't you dressed yet?"

"What?" I brushed the shoulder of my black jacket in a mock gesture of cleanliness. "I'm ready."

"That tired old thing?" Blix shook his head. "Besides being a worn-out cliché of space captain attire during the Zelfinian migration, when space drifters like you had their heyday, it's just plain drab. I mean, look at the rest of us." Blix spread his arms wide as if unveiling an art exhibit.

Blix wore his purple and gold ceremonial Vythian robes. They criss-crossed his muscular frame and held numerous rows of polished throwing knives.

Jasette was dressed in a shimmering black dress with pointed sleeve caps and intricate silver stitching throughout. Her smooth hair flowed over her shoulders. She looked incredible. I felt really lucky that she almost liked me.

Nelvan, on the other hand, was still wearing his silver jumpsuit.

"What about Nelvan?" I pointed at the boy, hoping to

deflect the negative fashion charges. "He's wearing the same old, outdated jumpsuit he came here in."

Blix shared a patronizing grin with Jasette. "Captain, silver jumpsuits are huge in Fantasmica right now. And Nelvan here has one made with old earth material from nearly a hundred gloons ago. It's one of a kind. He'll be talked about in all the fashion news tomorrow."

"Really?" Nelvan gave an amazed look at his jumpsuit, touching it gingerly as if afraid to damage it.

"Yeah well, who cares?" I plopped down in my captain's chair. "They don't like my clothes, they can go fly off a pulse tower."

As we descended from the clouds, a vast, shimmering city began to fill the screen. Skyscrapers came rushing toward us like an army of giants with crystalline spears. The high, pointed buildings were covered in mirrored surfaces. I saw my star freighter reflected in dozens of exterior building panels as we flew closer.

"Wow." Nelvan was staring wide-eyed at the viewing screen. "Everything's so shiny."

Blix nodded. "You never quite get used to the shimmering structures of Glittronium City."

Jasette scrunched up her face like something smelled rotten. "A lot of it is sim projection. See those spires over there?" She pointed to one of the taller, multi-spired buildings stabbing toward us. "Fake."

I gave her a questioning look. "You've been here before?"

She nodded. "Several times."

"Oh, I forgot. You're royalty." I gave a mock bow. "Of course you've been here to mingle with celebrities."

Jasette frowned. "I didn't say I liked it."

Blix moved close to Jasette and put a protective arm around her. "I think it's wonderful that you've traveled. It builds character. Unlike some people who stay in their dusty ships all day and never experience other cultures." Blix flicked his eyes toward me.

I shook my head. "Kissing up to phonies ain't experiencing other cultures."

"Well, it's better than—" Blix paused and looked up as if a new thought just came to him. His eyelids fluttered. "Oh my, we're in range of local thought strings. I'm getting instantaneous thought messages from major celebrities."

I grunted my disgust and hit the com panel on my armrest. "Glittronium port, this is star freighter GS1138 requesting docking."

A soft, rising series of harp-like tones came over the com link. A warm, pleasant female voice followed. "Welcome to Glittronium, GS1138. I'm Valladius, your landing guide. We've been tracking your descent and have reserved dock S23 in the luxury hangar for disembarking."

"Oh." I paused for a moment, not used to hearing the words *luxury* and *reserved for you* in conversations directed my way. "Really?"

"Of course," Valladius let out a small but courteous chuckle. "You're a special guest, Captain Starcrost. One of the five chosen competitors. And on behalf of the Glittronium welcoming committee, we wish you the best of luck."

The com link switched off with another series of harp tones. I looked at Jasette, still feeling a bit speechless.

She nodded as if impressed. "Looks like you're a bit of a celebrity yourself."

A slight shudder went through the ship. "Captain, can

you believe it?" Iris spoke in a delighted tone. "Luxury hangar accommodations. Oh Glint, this is wonderful."

"Just remember, I didn't do it." I'd been on my guard about gaining any accidental computer affections ever since Iris flipped out and nearly killed us all. "It's all Forglyn Sashmeyer, the pretty boy show host. He's the one that set all this up."

Of course, I had no idea who set up anything, but keeping things ultra platonic with life-system supporting supercomputers was now a priority in my handbook.

"Oh ..." Iris paused a moment. A few mismatched blips sounded. "Well, that was very hospitable of him. Please give him my thanks."

"You got it," I said.

A raised, mirrored pedestal with a crown of spires filled the viewing screen. We were headed for a wide, rectangular landing slip. Twin rows of blue path lights appeared to roll out from the slip to guide us in.

"Approaching the hangar, Captain." Iris said.

"Captain," Blix approached and spoke confidentially. "I recommend using a code word for the Emerald Enigma."

"Why?" I said.

"Audio sensors abound in Glittronium. Do you want it known that you have the Enigma?"

I nodded. "Right. Okay, just call it my charm. You know, kind of a double meaning. People will just think you're talking about how charming I am."

Blix raised a brow. "I don't think so. But not to worry, Nelvan and I have already discussed it. We'll call it—" Blix spread out his hands as if presenting a gift, "—your angel."

I frowned. "Not on your life."

"No, it's perfect," Blix said. "Just as the Enigma protects you, as the scriptures say, 'He shall give His angels charge over you, to keep you in all your ways.'"

Suddenly Jasette was at my arm. "Does that include giving him spider legs like the last Enigma owner?"

Blix shared a disappointed look with Nelvan. "She has a point. Perhaps we should call it your demon."

"I'm not calling it 'angel' or 'demon.' We're sticking with 'charm.'"

"How about 'temper?'" Jasette suggested. "People won't have any trouble believing that."

Blix gave a thoughtful look. "Indeed. Okay, we'll go with 'temper.'"

"We're almost there," Iris said. "Please head to landing bay for disembarking."

I stood and flashed an authoritative look. "I'm sticking with 'charm.'" I led the way to the lift. The doors chirped open and I motioned to Blix. "Take the kid first. I need to talk to Jasette."

"Ah." Blix looked from me to Jasette with a knowing nod. "Finally picked up on her obvious hints, did you?"

I made a commanding point to the lift. "In."

Blix winked at Jasette. "Come Nelvan, we mustn't disrupt the captain's maturity milestones, insignificant as they may appear at first glance."

Nelvan nodded and followed Blix into the lift. I gave Blix a good scowl as the doors chirped shut.

I turned to Jasette, trying to keep my composure non-threatening. "So ... how are you?"

She gave a slight shrug.

"You look nice. Your dress is really shimmery and everything."

Jasette paused as if I'd just asked her to rewire the ship computer. "That's a compliment, right?"

I sighed. "Okay, listen. I don't know what's going on with you. What's up?"

Jasette gave a casual shake of her head. "Nothing."

"Come on, you said you had something to tell me."

"I did." A slight fire returned to her eyes. "I don't want to talk about it right now."

The ship had slowed almost to a stop, nestling inside the polished, white-walled luxury hangar. I motioned to the slip on the viewing screen. "Look, soon we're gonna be at a noisy party filled with flashy phonies, and tomorrow I'll be in some insane competition where I might die, so we're running out of chances here."

She paused a moment, a crinkle line of concern forming between her eyebrows. "I have to leave."

I was prepared for the usual charges of things I'd done wrong, but not this. I opened my mouth for a response, but all that came out was a slight choking sound.

"The people of my kingdom are counting on me." She continued, realizing I was lacking any legitimate, utterable response. "I swore a mission to find the chrysolenthium flower. They're running out of time."

"Wait a freem. Didn't I tell you I'd help with that?" I fumbled. "The Enigma will help us find it."

"When? After the Iron Gauntlet—if you survive? I can't wait around on the off chance that happens." Jasette moved toward the lift doors. They slid open and she stepped inside.

"Hold on." I jumped in behind her as the doors closed

and the lift descended. "The competition doesn't last that long. Your kingdom has enough energy for another gloon."

"We think." Her expression was a mix of sadness and anger. "It could be less. I'm leaving right after tonight's reception."

"Listen, just give me a day to think about this. I'll come up with something."

Jasette softened a moment, the corner of her lip upturned in a slight smile. "I wish we had more time, Glint. I really do." She took a slow breath. "If you somehow manage to stay alive, find me in the Krennis sector near Jelmontaire. That's where I'll be."

The lift doors opened. She turned and headed down the hall toward the landing bay. All I could do was stand there and stare after her, wondering what I could possibly do to fix things.

CHAPTER 5

THE GLAMOUR
OF GLITTRONIUM

EVERY SURFACE IN THE LANDING BAY hanger was clean and white with a high gloss finish. The hanger was large enough to house a ship three times the size of mine. A few maintenance droids with glowing blue eyes were already hovering around my ship doing inspections.

I took a few tentative steps from the landing bay ramp onto the shiny floor. Luckily, my feet held fast. I wondered if the gloss was mere simulated luxury.

"Captain, this way." Blix motioned me over. He stood next to a hovering, crystalline sphere the size of an escape pod. Jasette and Nelvan were already sitting inside the sphere. They were sipping from elegant looking flutes filled with a sparkling, golden liquid.

I followed Blix into the sphere and took a seat next to Jasette. A clear, circular bench ran along the inner wall. The translucent door slid closed behind me and the sphere illuminated with a soft white glow. A thin orange track lit up underneath us, running a winding path from the hanger to a curving tunnel beyond. The sphere sped gracefully forward on the orange track, taking us on a circuitous journey through a glossy white tunnel. Two additional crystal flutes with golden liquid emerged from the table before us. Blix grabbed one and started sipping with his pinky finger raised high.

A hologram flickered to life from the table. The projection was a gorgeous woman with cascading red hair that looked like she'd stepped right out of a beautification orb. She was dressed in a stylish but official looking navy blue pantsuit. A large globe spun slowly in her open hand. It was a scaled down simulation of the planet Fantasmica with an incredible level of detail.

"Welcome to Fantasmica," the woman spoke in a velvety, smooth tone, "winner of the prestigious *Greatest Superplanet in the Universe Award* fifty gloons in a row." Fifty miniature golden trophies appeared and spun around the hologram planet like orbiting moons. "The highest percentage of famous beings in the universe are proud to call Fantasmica home. Many of them live right here in the exquisite city of Glittronium. Here are just a few of the reasons why." She touched the spinning globe and the visual zoomed in on the towering, reflective structures of Glittronium as if we were careening through the planet's atmosphere. "Take our world class spas for example ..."

As the woman droned on about exotic oil treatments I leaned over to Jasette. "Okay, how about this? You stick around for a couple of days, see how things go in the competition. If I'm doing well, you stay longer."

Jasette frowned. "And if you're dead?"

"Don't be so pessimistic."

"Shh!" Blix gave a disapproving scowl before turning his attention back to the hologram. "Nelvan, did she say vermillian steam bath or quintian?"

Nelvan had a studied expression. "Quintian, I think."

"Hey, I'm talking about real stuff here," I said. "Not some sissy spa."

Blix sighed and put a hand to his temple like he had a headache. "Captain, you really must get in touch with your feminine side. Besides, your conversation is pointless. If you spent any time analyzing Jasette's temperament, aspirations, and life experience, and how they fit into a highly predictable decision matrix, you'll realize her course is set. Your minimal powers of persuasion have no chance."

I grabbed one of Jasette's silver pistols and blasted the hologram table. The crystalline flute blew to pieces spraying the golden liquid on the walls as well as Blix and Nelvan. The hologram fizzled away. A dark, charred spot in the center of the table was all that remained.

"Bet your decision matrix didn't predict that."

I handed the gun back to Jasette, who didn't seem too pleased with its unauthorized use. Blix wiped the liquid from his face and flicked it to the floor like offended royalty. "Very mature, Captain."

"Not to mention rude." Nelvan tried to put a menacing look on his youthful face but it couldn't seem to take hold. It was as if he'd never used those facial muscles before.

Blix nodded at Nelvan and then leaned back and rubbed his temples. "I shall definitely need a deep scale smoothing treatment while we're here."

I turned to Jasette. "Help me out—there's gotta be a way you don't have to leave."

"Believe me Glint, I wish there was."

The tunnel came to an end, and the sphere emerged onto a broad, silver street lit with the golden Fantasmica sun. Glittronium was alive with activity. A multitude of tracks ribboned through the surrounding buildings, shuttling spheres identical to ours—filled with alien travelers—throughout the city. Most of the well-dressed citizens who walked the streets were humanoid, but as we glided deeper into Glittronium, a wider variety of life forms emerged. Everything from slithering worm giants to floating sprite convoys were making their way to the heart of the city.

"What a freak show." I watched the parade of aliens as we sped by. "Looks like this competition brings out all the weirdos."

"Are they dangerous?" Nelvan was scooting away from the window and closer to Blix at the sight of stingers, horns, and all means of alien ooze.

"Nothing to worry about, Nelvan." Blix gave him a reassuring pat on the shoulder. I let out a mocking laugh. Nelvan gave me an anxious look.

"Don't listen to him," Blix said. "We're on a highly civilized planet. Anyone visiting for the games will either keep their hostilities at bay or face the authorities of Glittronium. I hear they can be quite strict if the need arises."

Our sphere rounded a building and a towering, golden-hued structure appeared. It was about ten times the width and height of the surrounding skyscrapers. The top of it disappeared in the clouds overhead.

Nelvan let out a whistle. "I've never seen a building that big … or shiny."

"That's Shansmannor Hall." Blix craned his neck toward the edifice. "Perhaps not as colossal and daunting as the spiraling snail mounds of the Tendrif system, but for sheer manufactured elegance, it has no equal. An excellent choice for the competitors' reception."

"It's an over-glossed, bloated waste of space," I said. "All they ever use it for are stuffy celebrity parties and award ceremonies."

"Captain." Blix shook his head. "You're overplaying your disdain. It's obvious you're impressed on some level. Just admit it."

"I'll admit you're an idiot."

Blix hissed and narrowed his eyes.

"Would you two stop?" Jasette gave us a disapproving look. "We're almost there and you're not even discussing a game plan."

"For what?" I said. "The competition hasn't even started yet."

"Competitor research," Jasette said. "You need to learn everything you can about them before the game starts. Strengths, weaknesses, fears, impulsive behavior patterns. This is your one and only chance to do that."

I paused for a moment, wondering why I hadn't considered such an obvious course of action. "Well yeah, naturally that was my plan."

Jasette flashed me an annoyed look. "You can't mess around with a competition like this." She turned to Blix. "He's going to need your help."

"Princess Jasette, rest easy." Blix spoke in a formal tone. "The captain and I maintain a secret connection."

Blix closed his eyes and seemed to be concentrating. A series of vibrant communication icons spun into my head. The icons displayed a heroic, scaled creature defending a small man against a series of deadly looking aliens.

I let out a long sigh. "Are you through?"

Blix opened his eyes and smiled. "You see? Thought messages will be our secret correspondence."

"Was that supposed to be us?" I glared. "A giant lizard and a tiny man?"

"Sometimes thoughting is best left up to interpretation."

"Well, they're annoying. Save them for all your chatty celeb pals," I said. "Don't thought message me unless it's an absolute emergency."

Blix gave an exasperated look. "The Iron Gauntlet is a life-and-death competition; we'll be up to our scales in emergencies."

"Just use your communicator." I grabbed the communicator from my hip and waved it in front of his face.

"Fine." Blix glared at me then turned to Jasette. "It seems the captain wants to hamstring our advantages. Regardless, I've already viewed all the pregame segments on competitors and done extensive background research. The competition is fierce indeed, but I'm weighing counter measures."

Jasette patted Blix on the arm. "Thank you, Blix. I'm glad I can count on you."

The copper scales on Blix's cheeks went flush. "Oh, it's nothing. Such things are second nature for Vythians."

"Hey, what about me?" I said. "I'm the one competing

here. How about a little credit for the guy who might die, huh?"

Jasette turned to me, a sober look on her face. "That's why I can't stay around."

The sphere slowed to a stop as I searched my brain for a decent response. "Hey, don't worry. I've got my *charm*."

"Your *temper* is unpredictable," she said. "It doesn't offer much comfort."

The oval door of the sphere opened with a slick, whooshing sound.

"Welcome, Captain Starcrost and crew." The sun reflected off Shansmannor Hall, creating a golden-ringed silhouette of a shapely woman standing just outside. My eyes adjusted to the glare to find a curvaceous young lady in a custom-fitted, ice-blue blazer and pencil skirt. The outfit had an official look, but was off kilter as if she'd dressed in a hurry. Her hair shimmered with the latest weave technology. Glowing strands of blonde, pink, and lavender flowed with hypnotic rhythms through the wavy locks that cascaded to her shoulders. Several strands went astray from the rest and fell across her face like strong winds had undone a once-orderly hairstyle. Twitchy blinking animated her face as the loose strands seemed to tickle at her eyelashes. She brushed the strands aside with an embarrassed look and composed herself.

She waved a hand in front of her and a translucent blue holoscreen appeared and hovered in place. "I'm Selinxia, your concierge for the competition." She fixed me with bright blue eyes. Her pouty lips curled into a soft smile.

I hesitated, forgetting for a moment how to speak.

Jasette cleared her throat. "Wake up, Glint." She narrowed her eyes and stepped out of the sphere.

"Hello, you must be Jasette." Selinxia lightly kissed her fingertips and extended her hand in a customary Glittronium greeting. The courteous response was to swipe the fingertips with your own and place it to your lips.

Jasette returned the greeting in an obligatory manner.

Blix stepped out of the sphere and bowed. "Greetings, Selinxia. Your kind welcome is most appreciated." Blix exchanged the customary greeting and stood at attention with hands clasped loosely behind his back like some visiting dignitary.

"You're too kind," She said. "You must be Blix, the captain's first mate."

"Indeed."

Selinxia's eyes flashed back to me and her face lit up with a smile that could melt an ice planet. "Captain, won't you please join us?"

I found myself out of the sphere and standing in front of her, not knowing exactly how the process took place. "Glint Starcrost, at your service." Before I realized what I was doing, I broke into my old space academy salute. I crossed my arms over my chest and finished with a slight bow.

Selinxia gave a surprised little smile. "Why Captain, you are quite the debonair space explorer, aren't you?"

"I do what I can."

Jasette shook her head. "Really?"

I gave an apologetic shrug.

"Um, hi there." Nelvan was at my side, looking at Selinxia with wide-eyed wonderment.

"Welcome to Glittronium." She kissed her fingertips and offered them to Nelvan.

Nelvan stared blankly for a moment. I gave him a quick

nudge. He seemed to snap out of his daze long enough to reach out and shake her hand. She gave an amused look at his hand. "Well, to each their own custom, I suppose." She slid her hand away from Nelvan and tapped a few commands on her holoscreen. "I'm afraid I don't know enough about you to offer a proper greeting." She gave Nelvan an expectant look.

"Oh, I'm Nelvan." He put his hands on his hips and grinned. My guess was he was trying for heroic but it was a sad effort.

"I see." She tapped a few more controls on her screen. "Well, Nelvan, it will be my pleasure to get to know more about you. We like to understand our guests of honor better in order to make their stay here comfortable."

Nelvan gave an unsure look my way. "Yeah, okay."

"Great." She touched the screen and it disappeared. "The reception has already begun. We must be on our way."

She led me forward, and my crew followed close behind. We weaved through a crowd of finely dressed aliens as we neared the golden building.

Selinxia turned to me. "Is there anything you need for the competition, Captain?"

"Indeed." Blix emerged at Selinxia's opposite side before I could answer. "I'm curious as to whether your steam baths are vermillian or quintian in nature."

"I'm pretty sure they offer both," she said.

Blix gave an impressed nod. "I must say, Glittronium grows more cultured every time I visit. Now, about your cuisine, I'm wondering—"

"That's enough, Blix." I shot him a dark look. "She's talking about important competition supplies." I looked at Selinxia. "Do you have any insider info on the other contestants? You know, secret weaknesses, fears, that kind of thing?"

"Oh," She looked apologetic. "I'm afraid I don't really deal in that kind of information."

I shrugged. "I guess I'll just have to wing it."

The broad shadow of the golden edifice engulfed us as we neared the entrance.

CHAPTER 6

SHANSMANNOR HALL

THE FOYER OF SHANSMANNOR HALL was like being on the inside of a well-polished diamond. Glistening, triangular surfaces covered the walls and vaulted ceiling in a bedazzling geometric array. High recesses were accented with crystalline foliage that cascaded down the smooth walls, offering a nice contrast of texture.

"Shansmannor Hall has housed the most prestigious events of the last century." Selinxia spoke like a tour guide as she led me by the arm. "This is the base of operations for the most widely viewed shows in the universe, all major Glittronium elections and—perhaps most noteworthy—the daily award ceremonies for our major celebrities."

Blix let out a small gasp. "Speaking of celebrities. Isn't that Tellia Quinsmette, the actress/singer/dancer/award-winning humanitarian?" He pointed to a waifish-looking purple humanoid with silver hair in a clingy white dress.

"Tellia Quinsmette!" Selinxia let go of my arm, mesmerized. "I must say hello. No, I shouldn't. Should I?" She looked at me, hoping for guidance.

"Um, yes?" I offered.

Her face lit up. "Okay. I won't be a moment." She tried to adjust her outfit, then stumbled her way over to Tellia.

Jasette shook his head. "I'm guessing this is her first day."

I nodded. "Figures they'd stick me with a newbie."

A swarm of camera bots circled a couple nearby, clad in matching golden outfits.

Blix let out a low whistle. "This place is incredible. Everywhere you look, another star emerges."

"Kind of makes you feel self-conscious." Nelvan licked his palm and ran it over the side of his head to smooth his hair.

I didn't follow celebrity trends, but judging from the glitz and glamour of everyone in the foyer, the competitor reception netted quite a few of the current A-listers. A trio of slinky women in bright green dresses crossed my path. One of them shot me a seductive look as she passed by. She tossed her silky auburn hair as she gave me a second look and flashed a wicked smile. I wondered if my new position as a competitor was giving me some kind of celebrity status.

If women in Glittronium were drawn to that kind of thing, my time here might not be so bad after all.

Jasette cleared her throat. "Glint, are you going to be able to control yourself here?"

"What?" I tried to sound innocent.

She raised her eyebrows.

"Hey, they were looking at me. I barely looked back."

An unconvinced nod was her only reply.

"Okay look, I'm not used to all this." I motioned to all the surrounding glamour. "I'll keep things in check, I promise."

"You better." She gave me a playful slap on the cheek with just a hint of sting. "I'll be back. I need a drink." Jasette headed over to a moon-shaped counter filled with multi-colored beverages.

Blix held a hand to his temple. "Oh my."

"What? What's wrong?" I said.

"The celebrity thought messages are running swift and snarky today," he chuckled. "What marvelous entertainment."

I slugged him on the shoulder. "Would you knock that off? You're supposed to be helping me with strategic planning and competition prep."

Blix frowned and let out a slight hiss. "I've been doing that all morning. The Vythian mind, an intellect beyond your understanding, is nearly always engaged in deep thought. Occasionally, we need to give our mental faculties a break. Celebrity gossip is one of the most mindless sources of information available to facilitate mental rest."

I was about to launch into an attack on Vythian minds when a loud crash sounded near my head. I instinctively turned away as a spray of crystalline shards hit me in the side of the face. When I looked back, there was a large, metal mace studded with thick spikes lodged into a now-shattered wall beside me.

The owner of the mace was glaring down at me. He was a Vythian of slightly larger stature than Blix. He was decked out in an intimidating array of spike-studded metal and chain armor.

"A dire warning that, competitor," he said.

If a deep cave somehow learned how to talk, I imagined it would sound a lot like the Vythian warrior glaring down at me, except for an odd gurgle that punctuated the end of his threats.

He leveled a scaly finger at my forehead. "My way be

deadly fierce and ye best give way or suffer this mace through yer skull."

Nelvan gave a few desperate tugs at my jacket. "Captain, we should go."

The sudden shock of this unforeseen foe, combined with his barely restrained desire and obvious ability to crush me sent fear tremors down my legs. The impulse to beg for my life was very strong. Luckily Blix stepped in.

"You're from the Sclarbrontic Tribe, aren't you?" Blix seemed to be studying his dangerous armor as though reading runes on a wall. "Your dialect and armor patterns are clear marks of upper northwestern Vyth country."

The Vythian gave a slight flinch at the sight of Blix and then redoubled his scowl. "Who are ye? Name yer tribe and season."

"I am Blixorthuvan Cresventellioutte Felltuxious of the Evtherion Plains." Blix made two fists and hit them together above his chest in what looked like some kind of traditional greeting. "My season is one of battle although I'm currently at odds with cultural precedent."

The other Vythian paused for several long moments as if Blix had spoken another language. "I am Chakdragonnon Rekkdrukthix of the Upper Northern Drukthix." He paused again, still looking confused.

"Pleasure to meet you Chak," Blix said. "May I call you Chak? Full Vythian is a bit long winded."

Chak yanked his mace from the wall, lifted it up and made a slow rotation of his wrist so the spiked end swirled above Blix's head like a hypnotic ball of death. "Ye speak a strange tongue and my head be at pains. Me thinks it time to lock claw and scale in mortal combat."

"I should say not." Blix chuckled. "This is a civilized gathering."

Chak bared his twin rows of teeth and let out a low hiss. "Fight or die. That be yer choice." He raised his mace in a threatening manner.

"Nonsense." Blix grinned as though they were having a pleasant disagreement. "That is no choice whatsoever."

Chak let out a gurgle filled growl and swung the mace toward Blix. A triangle of golden beams shone on the Vythian and froze him in place. Three human-sized orb droids circled above, golden beams projecting from openings in their silver hulls.

"Violation seven point three nine," a digitized voice sounded from one of the droids. "Cease all hostilities at once."

"Don't speak to me of violations, robot." Chak's deep voice wavered.

The orb droids circled lower and the golden beams grew brighter.

The Vythian warrior hissed. "Prepare to suffer the wrath of a thousand vile serp—" His warning was cut short as he arched back with a painful grimace.

Selinxia rushed over and grabbed my shoulder. "What happened?" She looked from the Vythian to me in a panic. "Are you hurt?"

I shook my head, unable to look away from the frozen Vythian. He was writhing in pain, suspended in the golden lights. Obviously they didn't take security lightly in Glittronium. The droids hovered higher, lifting Chak in the air, suspended by the light. With a high-pitched whir, they ushered him from the room.

Blix shook his head. "They that live by the sword, die by

the sword." He looked at Nelvan. "It would do Chak well to heed the book of Matthew, eh Nelvan?"

Nelvan nodded, still wide-eyed from the confrontation.

"My apologies, Captain." Selinxia said. "I'll be sure to lodge a complaint with security."

"Lodge a complaint?" I shot her a confused look. "That's it? He could've killed me."

Her head tilted downward, her lower lip protruding. "I'm sorry, I'm kind of new at this."

"How new?"

"Brand new? Their main concierge team is busy with the other contestants. I was brought in from a third-party firm."

I gave Blix a defeated look.

Blix shrugged. "A bad day with a concierge is better than a good day without one."

He had a point. My life up to this point had been concierge-free. Having someone around to take care of you—even if they were inexperienced—didn't sound so bad. Plus, she was exceptionally easy on the eyes. I might as well enjoy a few days of living like a celebrity.

Selinxia patted my arm. "Come on, the reception is about to begin." She led me to a hexagon shaped doorway that opened to a darkened hall. "It's time for you to meet the host."

CHAPTER 7

THE COMPETITORS' RECEPTION

ENTERING THE MAIN ROOM of Shansmannor Hall was like stepping out of a starship in the middle of deep space—the expansive room seemed to have no end, all set against a black backdrop with countless pinpoints of twinkling light simulating stars at varying distances. The pathways that intertwined throughout the room were marked by colorful rings flowing around translucent planets. Guests mingled inside the colorful opaque planet domes or walked along the planet ring pathways like supernatural giants strolling around the universe unimpeded.

Nelvan gasped. "This place is incredible." I wanted to tell him it was no big deal, but I had to admit it was pretty impressive.

Selinxia led us down a luminous, curving ramp with a flowing, sand-like simulation. At the end of the ramp was a glowing sphere to give our path the illusion of traveling along a comet's tail. I felt a squeeze on my arm as she pointed ahead.

"Ah, there's the host now," she said.

Out of the rotating glow of the comet simulation emerged

Forglyn Sashmeyer. He headed toward us with a confident stride, the back glow of the comet casting a silhouette around him like a warrior returning from battle. Barely visible enhance bots flew above him, reflecting light across his chiseled features in complementary angles. He met us at the base of the ramp and offered the standard finger-kiss greeting to Selinxia.

"And who might you be?" Forglyn spoke in a deep, smooth voice.

"Greetings, Forglyn." She gave a shy smile. "I am Selinxia, Captain Starcrost's concierge."

"Really?" Forglyn leaned back, taking her in. "You must be new to the staff. I never forget a face, especially one so enchanting."

She let loose a nervous giggle that ended with a snort. "Yes, this is my first assignment."

"Wonderful," Forglyn said. "We must get to know each other better sometime."

They exchanged a nod as if acknowledging each other's abnormal beauty.

"And this must be the brave captain himself." Forglyn turned to me, hands on his hips. He gave me a scrutinizing once over, like an army general deciding if I was a fit soldier. "Glint Starcrost, one of the few human competitors that have dared set foot in the Iron Gauntlet."

I gave my best look of determination. "And soon the first human to ever win the game."

Forglyn gave an amused look. "Well said."

Selinxia touched my arm. "I have a few duties to attend to. I'll leave you in Forglyn's capable hands." She gave Forglyn a smile and headed deeper into the room.

Losing the company of Selinxia for Forglyn was definitely a downgrade.

"And here is your competitor bracelet." Forglyn handed me a clear, polished bracelet.

As I reached for the bracelet, Blix snatched it away.

"Beautiful." Blix was turning it over in his hand as if in admiration. "Is this refined cellis stone?"

"No." Forglyn frowned. "It's far more decorative than valuable."

"Well, it certainly is striking." Blix handed it back to me.

I grabbed it and gave him a scolding glance. I held it close to my wrist. As I looked for some type of latch, the bracelet became partially liquefied and wrapped around my wrist like a faceless snake.

"Just a bit of theatrics." Forglyn turned to Blix. "And you must be Blix. You may find it notable that one of our five competitors is Vythian."

"Yes," Blix said. "I believe we've met."

"Good, good." Forglyn retrieved another bracelet from a pouch at his side. "And here is your bracelet as part of the competitor's entourage."

"Wonderful." Blix took the bracelet and held it up, turning it to and fro before placing it on his wrist.

Forglyn cast an unsure look at Nelvan. "And … Nelvan, is it?"

Nelvan stepped forward. "Yes sir. Nelvan Flink."

"I hear you're quite the mystery man." Forglyn took on a playful tone. "We like to show a bit of history on our competitors' entourages but your past has proved quite elusive. You *will* tell us a few things, won't you?"

Nelvan gave an unsure look my way. I narrowed my eyes and gave the faintest shake of my head.

"Well," Nelvan said. "There's really not much to tell. I guess I just haven't done anything that would leave a historical record."

Forglyn gave a slow nod. "I see. Perhaps this game will change all that, eh?"

Nelvan gave a nervous grin. Forglyn handed him a bracelet but Blix snatched it up before he could take it.

I glared at Blix. "Would you stop doing that? It's really annoying." I grabbed the bracelet from his hand and gave it to Nelvan. "Here Nelvan, put this on."

Nelvan held it out to Blix. "You can have this one if you want. It's all the same to me."

Blix smiled and waved him off. Nelvan shrugged and put the bracelet on. Forglyn looked like he was about to say something but stopped, his attention focused behind us. I turned to see Jasette walking up to us.

"Hello, boys," Jasette said. "Miss me?"

"Well, well. Princess Jasette." Forglyn added an extra layer of suave to his voice. "It's been far too long."

Jasette nodded and gave a slight smile. "Hello Forglyn. You look well."

"You are too kind." He gave a slight bow. "And may I say you look even more exquisite than your last visit."

"You two know each other?" I said.

"I should say so." Forglyn chuckled. "We were quite an item for a while."

"A brief while," she clarified.

"Private cruises on my sky yacht ..." Forglyn looked

skyward as if lost in memory. "Fine dining in the gem gardens of Southern Fantasmica."

I turned to Jasette. "Funny you never mentioned it."

"It's not a big deal," she said.

Forglyn put a hand to his heart. "You wound me. I look on that time with fond memories."

Jasette huffed out a laugh. "It was great until your girlfriend showed up."

"It was all a simple misunderstanding."

"Ancient history." Jasette forced a smile. "I'm here for the reception and then I'm leaving."

"Not on my account, I hope. I'll set you up in the luxury suites." Forglyn spread his arms wide like a welcoming ambassador. "Consider it a vacation. Here, take this. The announcements are about to begin." He handed Jasette a bracelet.

Blix snatched the bracelet once again. I grabbed for it but he raised it out of my reach.

"What's wrong with you?" I gave Blix my angry eyes. "I told you to stop doing that."

"I can't help it," Blix said. "They're so beautiful."

"Give it to her now."

Blix hesitated a moment, then assumed a pouty look and handed it to Jasette. Jasette gave Blix a comforting pat on the back, then placed the bracelet on her wrist.

"Well, now that the preliminaries are taken care of," Forglyn said. "Let's begin."

A moon overhead shone bright and cast a spotlight down on Forglyn. A thin, glowing disc materialized beneath his feet and raised him slowly into the star field above.

A fist-sized, glowing audio orb floated toward him and stopped, hovering in front of his mouth. "Welcome." His voice boomed throughout the room in electronically amplified dominance. A simulated meteor shower streaked by behind him. "Welcome one and all to the 333rd Iron Gauntlet."

The room erupted in applause and cheers. A thunderous sound rose up as the crowds stomped their feet in rhythmic unison.

"Ah, the Iron Gauntlet death march," Blix said. "Even though it symbolizes the competitors marching to their death, it's actually quite stirring." I shot him a dark look.

A huge, three-dimensional hologram materialized in the center of the room. It was a finely crafted iron gauntlet. The gauntlet was closed in a dangerous-looking, upturned fist, accented by various spikes and angular carvings. The crowd cheered louder as it spun before them.

"Let me introduce the five worthy competitors." A pedestal lit brightly on the far side of the room. It illuminated a svelte alien with eight arms and a serpentine body. "May I present to you … Dentrylich!" Forglyn made a sweeping motion toward the alien. A series of comets streaked toward the serpentine creature and exploded around him in bright flashes of light. "Master of blades and three times champion of the agility death run."

As if on cue, Dentrylich drew eight curved blades and broke into a quick flurry of sweeping sword strikes. The crowd hooted and cheered.

"Our next competitor is known only as … Xi!" Another pedestal lit up by a simulated nebula. A floating, jelly-like substance undulated above the pedestal. "So toxic and deadly, mere contact with this being will bring more agony than Brenton Grivell's last movie."

The crowd erupted in laughter.

"Competitor number three puts the brute in brute force," Forglyn continued. "Let's give a warm welcome to … Chakdraggonon!" Another bright pedastal lit up under the large Vythian Chak. He swayed, looking a bit disoriented. He shielded his eyes from the lights and appeared confused. My guess was he still hadn't recovered from the effects of the holding rays.

Several multi-colored moons started orbiting Forglyn. "Now get ready folks, our fourth competitor comes all the way from the Vanthule Vortex. Here she is, the self-proclaimed wraith of the void … Chessandrillia!"

The fourth pedestal lit up but was completely unnecessary to showcase the bright form that hovered above it, a glowing, cloaked humanoid of dazzling white. Instead of hands, a myriad of luminous tendrils flowed out of the sleeves in slow, wave-like motions.

"Yikes," Blix said. "I'd watch out for that one, Captain."

"I'd watch out for all of them," Nelvan said.

"Better yet, study them," Jasette said. "Starting now, you need to learn these competitors before the game begins tomorrow. That's not much time."

"Don't worry," I waved a dismissive hand. "I've been all around this universe. I've seen worse."

Truth be told, I was terrified. My only plan was to stay as far away from them as I could.

"And our final competitor," Forglyn continued. "A surprise pick from the Iron Gauntlet supercomputer, may I present to you the surly, the gruff, the foul-tempered navigator of the stars … Captain Glint Starcrost!"

A bright pedestal lit up under me and lifted skyward. The sudden rush of attention made my stomach a little squirrely.

PAUL REGNIER

I felt like I should break into some kind of action pose to merit the focus of the room. But since my fighting skills were far more barroom brawl than martial artistry, I went for detached and mysterious. With my hands in my jacket pockets and a relaxed stance I put forward the confident, lone-wolf vibe. Only someone with powers unknown could portray such brash assurance in the face of visually superior competitors. At least, that was my best bluff.

"There they are, folks," Forglyn said. "A cast of competitors sure to amaze and surprise you. And speaking of surprises, we've equipped each of the competitor pedestals with high powered teleporters."

Several oohs and ahhs rippled through the crowd. My stomach churned at the word teleporter. No one had said anything about that twisted perversion of technology. I looked around to see if there was a safe exit from the raised pedestal. Unfortunately, the darkened floor below left too much mystery as to the level of injury I might sustain in the fall.

A white beam shot up from the base of the pedestal and my body went rigid.

"Get ready, folks," Forglyn spread his arms wide. A brilliant supernova lit up behind him and expanded outward. "The first surprise twist for this season of the Iron Gauntlet is that the competition starts *right now!*"

A strong wave of fear swept through me. The competition was starting early and I had no time to prepare. Not to mention the fact that I was still weaponless. I felt my body go light as the teleportation process activated.

CHAPTER 8

THE CHALLENGE OF
THE SHRIEKING WOMAN

MY VISION WAS SPOTTY for a few moments as the molecules of my body reassembled. The bright orange haze of an endless desert spread out before me. A disc of power residue still glowed beneath my feet. A repulsive odor hung in the air like badly burnt popcorn. For me, it was an obvious indicator of an unholy technology.

Distant hills on the horizon swam with heat waves. The four other competitors had materialized on the desert floor. We were spread out in a broad, circular formation. Luckily, there was a comfy distance between us. A narrow whirlwind of dust spun in the center of our crudely formed circle.

"The desert planet of Dothgurel." Forglyn's voice sounded small and digitized as it came through my competitor's bracelet. "Home to dire swarms of ancient dust worms." The dry, cracked earth rumbled as if to confirm his warning. "For centuries, the Blattonkoi tribe have used their vocal abilities to control the worms."

The dust whirlwind before us settled, revealing an old woman with scraggly white hair that exploded from her grey, weathered skin and deep-set black eyes staring blankly ahead. She raised her thin arms skyward, her badly fitted dress woven from some long dead-plant rustling in protest. A low tremor went through the ground.

"Competitors." Forglyn's voice took on a sense of urgency. "Behold the object of your challenge."

Five necklaces lit up around the woman's neck. At the end of each necklace hung a small, iron gauntlet. The cheers of the crowd sounded distant as the driving beat of the show's theme song urged us forward.

Chak made the first move. With a deep, guttural yell that still held traces of his odd gurgle, he ran toward the old woman. His grim, reptilian countenance communicated pure malice as he charged forward.

The old woman turned in his direction. She lowered one of her arms at him and opened her wrinkled mouth. A soft, high note sounded with a slow vibrato. Another rumble went through the earth.

The Vythian hissed as he drew near. The woman's voice grew stronger and became a piercing shriek. I clasped my hands to my ears as her voice rang in my head. The rumbling in the earth grew in force.

Chak closed in on the woman and raised his mace to strike. The ground before the woman exploded, and an enormous dust worm burst forth. It swallowed Chak whole as its white, bloated body emerged from the ground and arced overhead. A broad shadow spread out over the desert ground as its ascent reached its zenith. The worm's blubbery body rippled as it hung there a moment, then dove back into the ground like a fish returning to the ocean.

I took a few steps back at the gruesome sight, heaving as

the rancid odor of the unearthed worm hit me like a thick wind. A visual sweep of the area offered no hope for a safe retreat. There was nothing but flat desert in all directions and low hills far on the horizon.

The other competitors didn't seem to share my newfound fear of dust worms. They all advanced on the old woman in their own strange, slithering, hovering means of locomotion.

The woman raised her voice in a high shriek and the ground quaked. I clasped my ears in pain. It felt like someone was stabbing my eardrums. My eyes were squinted from the pain but I caught glimpses of multiple dust worms exploding from the ground around the woman and descending on the competitors.

The earthquake grew violent and I fell to my knees. Cracks in the dry earth around me began to widen. I felt the ground start to give way. I scrambled to my feet and leapt forward as a pit opened up beneath me. I grasped a crumbling ledge that offered a very temporary hold. My feet dangled over a wide chasm that descended into darkness. I tried desperately to get a better handhold, but the dry earth continued to crumble.

I craned my neck back. Something moved in the shadows of the pit. Something big. A jolt of fear surged through me, and I clawed furiously at the ledge to crawl my way out. The ground just crumbled within my hands as if to taunt my desperate efforts. All at once, I slid away from the ledge. The broad, bulbous, white head of a dust worm rose from the chasm below. I spun toward the hideous creature as it opened its huge, slimy maw. Trails of lingering mucus stretched from the ends of its wormy lips.

If only I could fly. This was a sad end to the semi-heroic exploits of a space captain.

A putrid blast of air from the advancing beast hit my face. I was only a freem away from becoming worm food. I instinctively threw my hands in front of my face just as a sharp pain erupted from my shoulder blades. I arched back in agony and somehow rose up from my slimy doom, emerging from the pit into the bright desert sky.

Something was pulling me with steady motion upward.

I looked back to discover long, bat-like wings flapping behind me. A chill went through me—some dark tunnel bat had latched onto me and was carrying me skyward. I doubted the bat creature had intentions of rescuing me— more like taking me away to some mountain bat nest to feed his hungry little bat children. The worm was apparently not too pleased with this new development, and it surged toward me and burst forth from the pit in an aerial lunge, its maw open wide.

I'll take the bat creature, I thought.

I looked back at the flapping wings, hoping my expression of wide-eyed fear would communicate our dire predicament, and in a burst of wing flaps we ascended high into the air.

The worm's bloated body was ill equipped for extended air travel and soon was arcing back into the earth. I let out a cry of victory as I hovered in the air, watching its descent. Far beneath me, I could still make out the stoic form of the old, grey woman. Sand worms were leaping and twisting around her, warding off the other competitors. Dentrylich, the eight-limbed serpent creature, was making some good headway. His eight blades were dancing skillfully across the bloated face of a wounded dust worm. I attempted a quick shift of body weight, hoping to wrench myself free of the bat's claws, but for all my effort, I merely changed position in the air, the creature matching my movement in perfect synchronicity.

Freedom wasn't coming easy. Judging by the tight sensation in my shoulder blades, his claws were dug in pretty deep.

A piercing scream came from below. Dentrylich had defeated the worm and was face-to-face with the woman, grasping at one of the necklaces. She was trying to fend him off with a short dagger as her worm minions were spiraling in. He grabbed one of the necklaces, and a teleportation disc lit up underneath him. In a bright flash, he vanished from sight.

The crowd's digitized cheers sounded from my bracelet.

"The first competitor has retrieved an iron gauntlet." Forglyn's voice rang out. "Dentrylich is now our leading contestant."

Another scream came from below. Chessandrillia, the wraith queen, was reaching toward the old woman with several glowing tendrils.

This is my chance, I thought. The old woman was completely distracted. If only this weird bat thing would fly me down there—and suddenly, as if in response to my thoughts, I dove toward the woman. The hot desert wind rushed over my face as I descended. I couldn't believe what was happening. Maybe I had some kind of psychic bond with this creature. I'd heard about these odd alien symbiotic connections in space bar tales but never really believed them.

I was starting to like this bat creature. Once I returned to Glittronium and got a laser pistol I'd have to blast it of course, but for now it was my best friend.

I was almost upon the old woman. I reached out to grab

the necklace just as she turned and spotted me. Her eyes narrowed and she let out a horrific shriek.

I cried out as my ears rang with pain. A huge worm burst from the ground in a shower of dust and dirt clods. It opened its slobbery maw wide to receive me. There was no time to slow my forward momentum, and so I careened through the slimy strands of mucus around its mouth straight into the worm's awaiting stomach.

CHAPTER 9

THE BELLY
OF THE BEAST

I THRASHED ABOUT in the pitch blackness, covered in slime. Everything I touched was bouncy and gushy, like being in a pile of oversized, mucus-covered pillows. The humid air of worm stomach put me on the verge of retching. This was definitely a low point in my life, trapped in a slimy cocoon about to be digested by a worm.

Suddenly my foot struck something hard. I would've cried out, but I didn't want a mouthful of mucus. After groping around my feet I discovered a large, metal plate, and desperate hope woke inside me that I had found something that could help me escape. After further examination, I felt several spikes sticking out of the metal. My hand ran across something softer and smoother, coated in slime. I'd cleared away a thick layer of gunk to get a better feel when it moved.

I tried to jump back but only managed to slip and fall into a fibrous wall. What had I awoken? If it was inside a hideous dust worm, it couldn't be good.

The moving thing spat and coughed several times. "Where am I?" it grunted. "What be this pit of filth?"

"Chak?" I recognized the voice of the Vythian competitor. "Is that you?"

"Who be askin'?" He spat a few more times.

"It's Captain Starcrost. We've been swallowed by a dust worm."

"Swallowed?" The Vythian hissed.

Everything sloshed and swayed for several moments as the Vythian growled and thrashed about.

"This grimy worm won't taste Vythian flesh today. Die you vile beast!"

The worm began to sway as Chak went into some kind of berserker frenzy, slashing through the flesh with his mace. A streak of sunlight broke through the darkness as the Vythian continued his onslaught. Finally the body of the worm heaved and fell away with a sickening, sloshing sound.

The old woman stood a few steps away from us, her face filled with shock. I sprang from the carcass of the creature and sprinted toward her. Chak leapt out beside me but his new slimy coating, coupled with his bulk, made for an unfortunate combination. He slid and landed on his side with a heavy thud.

Panic drove me forward until I was just steps away from the woman. Her face was a mix of fear and rage. She shrieked out her worm song, looking for one of her bloated guardians. With a final step I lunged for her. I couldn't be certain but it seemed the bat creature gave an extra thrust of its wings to speed my advance. My hand grasped a necklace as I collided with the woman, and I felt the welcoming jolt of a teleporter light up my molecules and send them packing.

CHAPTER 10

A Hero's Welcome

MAKING IT BACK to Shansmannor Hall in one piece, to the thunderous applause of the Iron Gauntlet audience, was one of the finer moments in my life. I was the second contestant to return, beaten only by the snaky swordsman, Dentrylich. Chak arrived a few freems after me, and our short-lived bond of being stuck in a dust worm's stomach together was shattered. He was enraged that I retrieved a necklace before him. He leveled his mace at my head and hissed a quick rant about crushing or smashing or some similar threat of demise. It was hard to tell through all the gurgling and hissing.

At the moment, his threats didn't matter. I was filled with relief at surviving the first challenge and too busy enjoying the extended cheers of the adoring crowd.

The stunned expressions of my crew were priceless.

"Wow, Captain." Nelvan was beaming. "That was awesome."

"You see?" Blix puffed out his chest like a proud father. "I told you he'd be fine."

Nelvan gave him a confused look. "Fine? You said his chances were so slim that—"

"Shh." Blix covered the boy's mouth.

Jasette ran into my arms and held me for a good five freem embrace. I was feeling really good until she broke our hug and slugged me on the shoulder.

"Don't ever get swallowed by a worm again." Her teary eyes gave me a scolding look. "You scared me to death."

I held up my hands. "Hey, trust me. It wasn't part of my plan."

She couldn't hold back a small grin and fell into my arms once more.

"Amazing." Blix turned to Nelvan. "Quite reminiscent of that Jonah and the great fish story you told me about."

I glared at Nelvan. "Boy, what have I told you?"

"He'd already read it." Nelvan pointed at Blix as if to deflect the charge. "I only answered a few questions he had."

"Blast it! Stop reading that book," I said.

"What book?" Blix tried to play innocent.

I was about to launch into more scolding when Jasette turned my face back to her. "Worry about that later." She wiped a few remnants of slime from my face. "Let's just enjoy this moment."

The crowd nearby clapped at our reunion. All things considered, Jasette was at my side and a crowd was cheering for me. For the moment, life was good.

I was just starting to revel in my victory when I felt the strange sensation of flapping at my back. The bat creature!

I grabbed Jasette by the shoulders and fixed her with a resolute stare. "There's a bat creature on me. When I turn around, blast it."

With a quick spin, I braced for the residual shock of her laser blast.

"Um, Glint?" Jasette said.

"What are you waiting for?" I said. "Blast it!"

"I can't."

"Why?"

She paused. "Because the wings are a part of you."

It took several moments for her words to sink in. As I reached back to my shoulder blades, my fingers discovered the awful truth.

A hesitant glance back revealed the end of a black wing in a relaxed position. I took a slow breath and thought about flapping—and the wings responded instantly with a strong flap. A gust of wind tousled my hair.

I turned back to Jasette, speechless. She looked like she didn't know whether to console me or laugh. She flicked her eyes to my chest, where the Enigma lay hidden under my shirt, then back at me. "I told you to get rid of that *temper* of yours." A sinking feeling went through me at the thought of what else the Enigma might do to me. Every day I wore it was another chance for some freaky mutation to take hold. Even though it seemed to be a safeguard of sorts, I was starting to think the risk wasn't worth it.

"Well, well, well ..." Forglyn strode up to me. The moon spotlight bathed us in soft, white light. "It looks like our second contestant has just flown in from the challenge." He spoke in full show-host cheesiness. "I'm beginning to see why the Iron Gauntlet supercomputer chose him." He crinkled his nose and waved a hand in front of his face. "Whew. Those of you watching with aroma vision might want to deactivate your sensors. Time in the belly of a dust worm has left the captain in dire need of a cleansing cube."

The crowd laughed as Forglyn turned on his heel and headed toward Chak. "Let's go check in with our Vythian friend, the third to arrive."

He walked away and the moon spotlight followed behind.

"Congratulations, Captain." Selinxia stood behind my crew, her blue holoscreen hovering at the ready. "Here, I figured you'd want this." Selinxia handed me a heated towel.

"Thanks." I took the towel and wiped down my face and hair. Soon it resembled a giant's handkerchief after a gruesome sneeze. I held it by my fingers for a moment, not sure where to put it. Selinxia hit a control on her holoscreen and a small, spherical droid flew over, hovering directly underneath the towel. She motioned to the droid, and I let the towel fall over its shiny, metal head. It let out a few discordant beeps before zipping out of the room.

"Follow me," Selinxia said. "I'll take you to the luxury suites. I trust you'll find them to your satisfaction." She turned and headed into the crowd.

I raised my eyebrows at Jasette. "Luxury suites?"

She smiled and patted my arm. "Not bad."

Blix clasped his hands and looked up. "Please let there be scale smoothing treatments. Please let there be scale smoothing treatments."

CHAPTER 11

THE 444TH FLOOR

SELINXIA TOOK US up to the 444th floor of Shansmannor Hall in a frightening contraption called a transverse cube. She insisted it wasn't teleportation and went into a lengthy explanation about velocity and matter exchange rates and how it was safe and tested and guaranteed and a lot of other assurances I had zero trust in. The clear transverse cube arrived at our floor in an impossibly short amount of time and slid us out like meat ready to be packaged and sold. I felt all wobbly inside. Because of the harrowing challenge I'd just been through, I couldn't pin the feeling directly on the cube but my strong hunch was to give it full blame.

Selinxia led the way down a luxurious hallway while Blix droned on about the conveniences of modern technology. We were surrounded by ornate, marble columns and ivory statues of various muscular creatures carved in athletic poses. A sim vaulted ceiling was covered in masterful paintings. The scenes depicted all manner of alien combatants locked in mortal combat.

She reached a shimmering golden door with the number 4444 etched into the metal and turned to face us. "This is your room. Cleansing facilities and fresh clothes are inside. I'd imagine you'd like to get cleaned up." I glanced down at the partially dried coating of worm slime that still hung on my clothes.

"Yes, Captain." Blix gave me a disgusted look. "The sooner the better."

"Your bracelet will give you access." Selinxia turned to the others. "If the rest of you will follow me, your rooms are just down the hall."

Jasette patted me on the shoulder and leaned close. "I'll come back and check on you. We can talk then." She gave a soft smile and headed down the hall with the others.

Perhaps my brush with death had broken down the wall between us. I couldn't really blame her for acting distant earlier. She felt she had to leave to save her kingdom and didn't want to watch me risk my life in this contest. It was nice to have someone who cared nearby, especially when I had a group of other competitors who wanted me dead. I hoped I could convince her to stick around for a little longer, without mentioning my risky deal with Parallax. The last thing I wanted to do was put her in danger.

All the possible arguments I could use to make her stay spun through my mind as I watched her head down the hallway. I prided myself in the fact that I wasn't merely watching her walk away in a form-fitting ceremony dress for the mere visual enjoyment, I was actually thinking meaningful thoughts about our relationship.

It almost bordered on maturity.

With her woman's sixth sense she looked back and caught me watching. She flashed a knowing smile before turning back to follow the others. I gave a contented sigh at the thought of us and touched my bracelet to the golden door.

There was a soft click and the door dematerialized. I stepped into an expansive room that was well beyond my means to afford, even for a night. The palatial marble and column framed décor from the hallway continued throughout my room, with finely painted murals covering the walls, depicting muscular, weapon-wielding combatants in heroic poses. Soft harp music flowed, and the sim vaulted ceiling displayed a series of silver framed windows with puffy clouds drifting overhead. All around lay large silken pillows, with ivory statues of majestic creatures gracing the tops of round marble tables. One of the walls was a full-length window that showcased the impressive cloud-level view of the city. "Hello, sir," a rich voice filled with refined, courteous programming came from the ceiling. "My name is Jenson. I am here to accommodate your stay to the best of my abilities. How may I be of service?"

I looked around the palatial room, wondering what I could ask for that wasn't already there. "It smells like soap in here."

"Quite right, sir," Jenson said. "My apologies. Do you have a preferred scent?"

"Cinnamon?"

The faintest hint of cinnamon wafted through the air. I breathed deep and felt my body relax. "Not bad. You got any velrys?"

"Only the choicest blend, sir."

A pedestal rose from the floor before me with a steaming cup of velrys.

I grabbed the cup and took a sip. It was smooth and perfect. I decided my stay here wouldn't be so bad after all.

CHAPTER 12

NIGHT VISITOR

WHEN I STEPPED OUT of the cleansing cube, my clothes were cleaned and neatly folded on a silken pillow. Small droids had scuttled out of the walls the moment my clothes hit the floor and whisked them away, so it didn't come as that much of a shock. I pulled on my trademark dark captain's pants with a thick solar strip down the side. It had been a task taking off my jacket and shirt with my strange new wings, and I was wondering how I would slip them back on when a high tone sounded.

"Terribly sorry to bother you, sir," Jenson said. "But you have a visitor."

I grabbed my shirt and headed for the door. Apparently Jasette wanted to talk sooner than I expected. I hadn't formulated a convincing speech to make her stay, but it would be nice to have help getting my shirt back on.

I waved my bracelet over the door control panel. The golden door dissolved, and I was surprised to find Selinxia standing there. She wore a tight, silver dress with a pulsating radiance as if it were cascading around her. Her shimmer-weave hair flowed with silver and blonde strands, gathered up in a complicated-looking spiral with a few loose curls that framed her face nicely.

"I hope I'm not disturbing you." She smiled with freshly glossed lips. "A package for you arrived at the service desk." She held forth a silver box topped with a white ribbon.

"Oh … thanks." I took the box, confused. There was a small tag on the top that read,

A gift.—Silvet

My mind raced. More vibe spheres? I couldn't open the box in front of Selinxia, so I set it on the entry table like it was no big deal. Selinxia's eyes lingered on my torso for a moment. "I can see why you're gaining favor votes from our female viewers."

"Really?" I had no idea what favor votes were but it sounded good.

She smiled and nodded. "That's an unusual necklace."

I froze, realizing she was looking at the Emerald Enigma hanging uncovered from my neck.

My mind went into emergency tale spinning mode. "It was my father's. It's more sentimental than anything of value." I gave a casual shrug as if embarrassed to wear a worthless necklace. "He gave it to me as a child. We never had much money so it's probably not worth its weight in vibes." Selinxia shared a polite laugh that assured she'd bought the bogus memory. "Still—" I gave a dramatic and sentimental look at the stone, "it reminds me of him so I never take it off."

When I looked back up, her eyes were moist. She placed a hand on her heart. "That's beautiful." I gave a sad little smile. I felt a twinge of guilt at being such a good liar, but it was a necessary evil at the moment. "I'm on my way to the after party. I thought you might like to, um, maybe come with me?" She gave a nervous look at the floor. "Of course, you'd be a guest of honor."

"Oh, actually …" Suddenly I couldn't think of a reason not to go. My mind was very fuzzy at the moment. "Did you say guest of honor?"

"I can wait if you'd like. I mean, so you can get dressed." She blushed.

"Hmm, well, maybe. I don't have to wear anything fancy, do I?"

"No. I'm probably overdressed. Do you think this is too much?" She spun around, revealing the deep scoop of her backless dress. Despite her newbie abilities as a concierge, she could sure look good when she wanted to.

"N-no. You look great."

She beamed. "Thanks."

"Yeah, that's quite a dress." Jasette suddenly appeared in the hallway behind Selinxia. She was back in her power suit with her arms folded over her chest. Her wide stance indicated she was either relaxed or about to throw roundhouse kicks. Obviously she'd heard at least part of the conversation and I could tell by her detached expression I was already tried and condemned.

"Oh, hello Jasette." Selinxia gave an awkward turn to Jasette. Her arms were all fidgety as if she didn't know what to do with them. "Um, you know there's an after party tonight? And—"

"So I hear." Jasette kept her focus on me. "A word?" She headed past me into the room.

Selinxia wore a guilty look. "I didn't mean to cause any trouble."

I shook my head. "Don't worry about it. I'm sure once I explain what happened we'll laugh about this later."

I knew there would never be laughter about this moment.

"Well, I'd better be going. It's in room number one if you want to go." She gave a nervous smile and left.

My body tensed as I turned to Jasette, preparing for the onslaught. "Nothing's going on, we were just talking."

Jasette gave a laugh that sounded more like the snort of an angry bull. "Yeah, I can see that." She looked at my shirtless condition and raised an eyebrow.

As if to add insult to my already awkward situation, my sudden desire to be wearing a shirt somehow prompted my new wings to wrap around my torso like a blanket.

She chuckled. "Now that's just sad."

"I just got cleaned up. I thought it was you at the door. I needed help to get my shirt over my … *wings*." It felt horrible to refer to them as *my wings*.

"If you're not ready for an exclusive relationship, that's fine with me." Jasette said.

I waited for a few moments for the punch line. When nothing followed, I tried a response. "Really?"

She nodded, her face void of expression. "Sure. If you want to drool at every pretty thing that gives you attention, that tells me all I need to know. I'd rather not waste my time with you."

"Wait a freem, you're acting like I did something. She was the one being all flirty." I pointed at the empty hallway as if Selinxia was still standing there. "All I did was think about going to that party where I'm some kind of guest of honor."

She gave an unconvinced nod.

"Look, nothing's going on with Selinxia. I mean, she's amazing looking and everything, but that doesn't matter."

Jasette's eyes narrowed. "You think she's amazing looking?"

"Well, yeah ... I mean, no. Not really. Not compared to you."

She shook her head. "Where did you learn to talk to women?"

"Okay, I'm not smooth. I get it. All I know is that you're the one I want to be with."

Jasette took a few deep breaths and seemed to relax a little. She took a step closer and took my hand in hers. "Glint, we've been through a lot in a short time. I'd be lying if I said I didn't have feelings for you but life is short, especially the crazy lives we've chosen to live. I need something real. Something lasting. Or at least, something with those intentions."

The conversation had taken a swift turn into the danger zone. My maturity levels were fighting to stay afloat. I searched for words but they weren't coming easy. A simple thought rose to the surface. "Jasette, I don't want to lose you."

She smiled and squeezed my hand. "I know there's a sweet guy in there. He's the one I'd like to know better. Maybe we just need some time apart so you can decide who you want to be."

The thought of time apart hit me harder than I expected. "Listen, maybe I don't have all the right words to explain things. I just escaped the slime-filled stomach of a giant worm. Do you know what that does to a guy?"

"There's a transport leaving in the morning for Blendark 9.

That's where I left my cruiser before I teleported to your ship and took control of it."

"*Almost* took control."

"Semantics," She grinned. "Anyway, I have to get back to the search to help my kingdom. Forglyn is arranging the free transport. I'm meeting him for breakfast to discuss the details."

My mind hung on the words *Forglyn* and *breakfast*. I let go of her hand and took a step back. "Wait, that pompous showboat is offering you free transport and having breakfast with you?" I gave her a challenging stare. "That's worse than anything I've done. You guys used to date."

She shook her head. "There's a big difference. He's a creep and I'm not interested in him."

"But what if he's interested in you? What if you go to his glitzy, giganto room and he lures you in with his shiny suits and sparkly eyes?"

Jasette put her hands on her hips and struck a challenging pose. "I think I can handle myself."

"He's a professional schmoozer. He'll start throwing evening gowns and diamonds at you. You'll get all confused."

Her angry eyes flashed. "Do you really think I'm that stupid?"

"Hey, you're the one having breakfast with him." The words were out of my mouth quicker than I could stuff them back in.

She sighed and turned, heading for the door. "Okay, I've had enough."

"Wait, Jasette," I said.

"I'm glad we talked," she said without turning back. "Makes my decision so much easier."

Her footsteps disappeared down the hall. I imagined my trusty old DEMOTER in hand, blasting Forglyn into oblivion. It helped to alleviate the anger a little.

I stood there for a moment, not sure what to do next. This was all new territory for me. I was used to the life of a lonely space drifter, and suddenly I was being thrust into serious relationship discussions and the limelight of a popular but deadly competition. Throw me into a dingy space bar filled with star pirates and interstellar thugs and I know what to do and say. But here, I had no footing. So far, I was succeeding in a high-stakes competition, people were cheering for me, and beautiful women were actually speaking to me without calling me 'creep' at the end of the conversation. I felt very out of place.

I wondered if I should just call it a day. After all, I was pretty beat from all the stress and craziness of the challenge, and the suite had a cushioned hover sleeper with massaging pulsators calling my name. It was tempting to just lie down and let the day end. But I couldn't leave things with Jasette the way they were.

I spread out my shirt, wondering how I would put it on. I noticed it had been stitched where the wings broke through. Not only that but there were custom wing slots tailored into the material.

I threw it over my head and concentrated on flattening the wings against my back. There were a few moments of flapping and frustration, but once I worked out the finer points of wing control, my shirt was in place.

I went back to retrieve my black jacket and found it was similarly tailored to allow for the wings. Although I hated to see my prized jacket torn, it was a sad necessity considering my freakish condition.

I stepped into my boots and headed out of the room. A brief trip down the hallway took me to room 4443, Jasette's room.

I activated the guest alert panel and knocked for several moments but there was no response. Nelvan emerged from the next door down the hallway. He waved happily and headed over.

"Hey, Captain," Nelvan said. "Man, you really did great today. You and that *temper* of yours." He looked toward my chest.

I frowned. The temper reference was sticking. "Thanks, kid. You seen Jasette?"

"She's probably at the after party. That's where I'm headed."

"Wait, you're going to the party?" I said.

"Yep. We're supposed to be guests of honor." Nelvan smoothed his jumpsuit. "This is pretty exciting. I've never been anywhere this nice."

I looked around at the decadent décor in a hallway nicer than most homes I'd seen. "That makes two of us."

"It's hard not to get caught up in it." Nelvan shook his head as if waking from a nap. "I have to keep reminding myself of that scripture, 'The things which are seen are temporary, but the things which are not seen are eternal.'"

It was a little ethereal sounding, but anything that chipped away at the facade of Glittronium was good with me. "Yeah, and half of it is sim projection."

Nelvan nodded. "Don't worry, Captain. I'm keeping my

wits and praying for you. This is dangerous stuff. After Xi got eaten by that worm, I knew nobody was safe."

"Wait. What? Who got eaten?"

"Xi. Y'know, that weird, floating jelly thing."

"I thought he—it—was toxic."

Nelvan shrugged. "I guess not to dust worms."

It was a sobering thought. It reminded me how close I came to a similar fate.

Nelvan glanced down at the communicator on his hip. A glowing green band of light was circling around it. He grabbed it and brought it to his face. "Hey Blix. Okay, on my way." He looked back to me, excitement in his eyes. "They're about to start the laser show."

Nelvan hurried down the hallway, motioning for me to follow.

"I'll catch up with you," I called after him.

The boy'd given me an idea. I grabbed my communicator and sent a signal to Jasette. The red band swirled around it several times to indicate it wasn't being answered. I headed back down the hallway, defeated. I doubted she was at the party, but it was the only other place I knew to check. As I passed by my room, I noticed the door was open. I distinctly remembered it rematerializing after I left. I peeked in, figuring the cleaning crew was there.

The lighting looked like it had been switched to sleep settings. Subdued, ice blue lights shone on the statues and tables throughout the room. A distant star field blinked overhead on the sim ceiling.

"Hello?" I called into the room. "Anyone in here?"

The room remained quiet. The soothing music and light cinnamon aroma were missing as well.

"Jenson, bright lights up to maximum," I said.

Nothing changed. Either the vocal responders were out or my room controls were just plain broken. I walked over to the touch panel on the far wall to access manual operations. The steel colored Iron Gauntlet logo was spinning on the screen in all its shiny, three-dimensional glory. I tapped at the screen to bring up the controls. The logo continued its slow spin, taunting me with its unresponsiveness. For such a swanky, luxury suite, you'd think things would be working better. It just confirmed my belief that technology was always a gamble.

I hit the front desk panel beside the screen. "My room controls are down. Can you send someone up here?"

No response.

I rested my hand on the communicator at my hip. I thought for a moment about calling Blix, but I pictured him rushing up to my room and finding nothing but my overactive imagination. He'd give me some lecture about me being overstressed and that I needed a spa treatment or some nonsense. I let the communicator go and shook off the feeling.

I hit the panel a few more times. "Hey, can anyone hear me?"

"I keeeen heeeear you." A voice came from hallway leading to the sleeping chamber. It sounded like someone speaking through a tube mixed with claws scraping against metal.

I spun to find a bulky, metallic figure standing in the shadows of the hall. He took a few steps forward, his heavy footfalls clanking their advance.

A flash of panic hit me. I instinctively reached for my DEMOTER, only to be greeted by the empty holster once more.

A cyborg emerged from the hall, his form ghostly in the blue light. Mismatched metal plating covered his body with badly burnt skin peeking out between the gaps. Tufts of blonde hair poked out from the spaces in his lopsided metal plated head. A glowing band of red light shone out from a cavity in the metal head where the eyes should be.

Since his face was covered in metal, it was impossible to guess what his expression was but I had the unshakable feeling he wanted to crush me into very small pieces.

CHAPTER 13

CYBORG ATTACK

MAN, HOW I HATED CYBORGS. They were a prime example of technology gone wrong. Unpredictable, dangerous and always with a chip on their shoulder.

The bulky machine pointed a thick, metal finger at me. "Gleeent Steercroooost."

"Who?" I said.

"I am heeeere to cooooollect." Rocket boots ignited under his feet in a bright, pulsating orange and lifted him a few inches off the ground.

I took a few steps back, fear pulsating through me. "Listen, you got the wrong guy. My name is Nelvan and—"

"Coooollect!" The cyborg rocketed toward me, hands reaching forward.

I dove sideways. Something horribly solid clipped my shoulder and sent me to the floor in an awkward spin. I rolled to my side and signaled Blix on my communicator.

The cyborg banked off the windowed wall and circled back in a well-controlled spin. He hovered there for a moment as if getting his bearings.

My heart was flying. All I could think about was getting out of there. Fast. On a table beside me was an ivory statue of a winged horse in flight. I sprang to my feet, grabbed the statue, and hoisted it over my head.

A plate on his shoulder slid away and a metal barrel rose up and shot an orange beam toward me. There was a terrific, crashing sound as the beam obliterated the winged horse statue and my hands trembled with the impact. A shower of white marble dust poured over me like an unlucky snowfall.

"Yoouu aarrre coomiiing weeeeth meeee." The cyborg hovered slowly forward.

"Over my dead body." It was an impulsive and unfortunate response on my part. Saying something like that to an off-balance cyborg was more of a delightful offer than a threat.

"Here, catch." I threw my communicator at his head and bolted toward the open doorway. The sound of his rocket boots drew close as I ran. I could tell he would reach me before I made it to the door.

Desperation stirred my wings into action. Suddenly I was flying through the room. There was a confused sounding grunt as the cyborg collided with me. We crumpled to the ground in a painful roll. I smashed into the entry table and something silver fell on my head.

There was a distinct taste of blood in my mouth. Hopefully all my teeth were still in place. The cyborg stirred on the ground several feet away from me, so I grabbed the silver box that had landed on my head—the present Selinxia gave me from Silvet. The top of the box had come loose and a shiny metallic object lay within. I was about to open it when the cyborg rose up. His eye band flashed red as he spotted me.

A metallic cable shot out from the palm of his hand and wrapped around my ankle. He gave a forceful yank, and a shot of pain went up my leg as I slid across the marble floor toward him.

I clung to the silver present and yanked the top free. Inside was one of the most beautiful sights I'd ever seen. Nestled on crushed black velvet was a titanium-plated DEMOTER X, the elite, limited edition of the y-series DEMOTER pistols. My mouth hung open at the glorious sight.

"Cooollect!" The cyborg gave another harsh tug at the cable. Another shock of pain radiated from my ankle as he pulled me within arm's distance. The red band across his head was glowing brightly. He retracted the metal cable and leaned forward, his metal fingers reaching for me.

I grabbed the DEMOTER and heard the triumphant whir of destructive energy as I powered it to full.

"Say goodbye, freak." I squeezed the trigger and a bright blast of white energy blew the cyborg across the room. He smashed against the full-length exterior window, and a few, thin cracks in the glass rippled outward from the impact. I decided the cyborg should learn how to freefall from the 444th floor.

I sent a series of rapid-fire DEMOTER blasts into the window behind him. As thick as it was, the blunt force of my new weapon turned it into a spider web of deep cracks.

The cyborg struggled to his feet, swaying as he tried to regain his composure. I extended the DEMOTER toward him, held firmly in both hands. I grinned and gave a tight squeeze on the trigger.

The bright energy blast hit him square in the chest and blew him through the huge window in a thunderclap of shattered glass. There was a descending, metallic echo that I guessed was his version of a scream. His cry faded away as he took the long plunge toward a well-earned demise.

The sound of hurried footsteps came from the hallway. Blix arrived at the door with several security guards dressed in stylish black uniforms with gold accents.

"Oh, now you show up." I threw up my hands in exasperation.

Blix glanced around the disheveled room. "What happened?"

I stuffed the DEMOTER X in my holster. It fit like an old glove. "I almost got killed. Some unhinged cyborg came after me."

Blix moved toward me, his face a mask of concern. "How? Did he come through the window?"

"No, but he sure left that way." I turned to the security guards. "Hey, what's with the security around here? I get attacked in my room the first night?"

The guards exchanged worried glances as if they all might get fired for the event. One with a well-trimmed black goatee and perfect teeth stepped forward. His forearm was wrapped in a form fitting silver computer. He gave a conciliatory bow.

"Sir, I am officer Grilg. Shansmannor Hall offers their deepest apologies for—"

"Save the rehearsed speech," I barked. "What happened to my top level security?" Grilg tapped out a few commands on his forearm computer. The lights in the room came back on and an ascending whir of systems powered up. "Sir ..." He looked at a loss for words. "Unauthorized room entry is highly irregular. Our scanning systems are very thorough."

"Not thorough enough, obviously."

Grilg look embarrassed. "Yes, well I—"

"Captain Starcrost," Jenson, the room computer broke in. "Please tell me you're alright. I was deactivated. I see signs of a struggle. Oh, heavens, it's all my fault, isn't it? Please tell me what I can do to fix things. I can draw a hot bath and prepare gourmet—"

Grilg hit a few controls and Jenson powered off. "Sorry. Our room computers can get a bit territorial. Now, can you tell me exactly what happened?"

"Well, for starters, my *luxury room* controls were broken." I made a sweeping motion to condemn the whole room. "Then some cyborg who was hiding out in my room ambushed me."

A crinkle line of concern formed between his eyes. "An evil cyborg?"

"Is there another kind?"

Grilg frowned and turned to the guards. "Get two squads on security sweeps."

The guards nodded and rushed out of the room. Grilg tapped out a few more commands.

"Grilg, I must say I'm quite concerned." Blix spoke with a full helping of diplomatic courtesy. "Shansmannor is well touted for their safety. How could such a thing happen?"

"A thousand apologies, sir." Grilg made a supplicating gesture, his face animated with a nervous smile. Obviously he was more intimidated by Blix than me. "I will do my best to get to the bottom of this immediately."

A soft whir came from the hallway. A dozen fist-sized sphere droids hovered into the room.

Grilg turned to the droids. "Thorough sweep. I want triple redundancy and cross bio segmentation analysis."

The droids immediately set to work. They hovered

through the room in frenetic flight paths. Their green scanning rays swept the furniture and walls in an industrious whirl of robotic efficiency.

Blix touched the corner of my mouth. When he pulled back his hand, his finger had a smear of blood on it. He showed the finger to Grilg who flinched as it came near. "I believe the captain needs medical."

Grilg nodded vigorously. "Yes, of course, sir."

"I don't need medical." I felt fine, but my adrenalin had been running so high I hadn't considered injuries. I did a quick check of my body to make sure there were no bloody gashes or missing limbs.

Blix waved off my protest.

Selinxia arrived at the doorway, out of breath. When she spotted me, she put a hand to her chest and exhaled in relief. "Thank goodness you're all right. I heard you were attacked."

"Yeah, no thanks to security." I motioned to Grilg with my thumb. He gave an embarrassed look down and busied himself with his computer.

She stood up straight and straightened her dress. "This is unacceptable. I shall lodge a complaint immediately."

I shared a defeated look with Blix.

She turned to Grilg. "You. Guard person. I, um, demand more security for Glint."

He gave her a confused look. "Who are you?"

"I'm Selinxia." She put her chin up. "Glint's personal concierge."

Grilg looked like he was trying to hold back a smile. "I see. Well, in that case, the security of Shansmannor Hall offers their deepest apologies and will do their utmost to address your concerns." He ended with a slight bow.

Selinxia nodded. "Great." She turned to me, looking triumphant. "Well, that should take care of things."

"Yeah." I forced a grin. "Thanks a bunch."

She gave a confident turn on her heel and headed off.

Blix patted me on the shoulder. "She means well."

A group of white uniformed people arrived at the door. They were carrying a host of expensive looking medical gadgetry and were flanked by droid assistants.

Grilg turned to them. "Examine the captain and report to me at once."

They nodded and rushed toward me like attackers.

For the next trid or so my room was busy, with sphere droids scanning every nook and cranny and various medical staff and their robot assistants rushing in and out of the room. They ran endless tests on me and asked me the same questions over and over about how I was feeling and does this hurt or does that hurt until I'd had enough and threw them all out. Jenson, my room computer, spent the entire time apologizing and saying the security breach was somehow his fault and how it would never happen again. It went on and on like this until I ordered him to shut up for the remainder of the night.

I had a headache from all the commotion but didn't dare mention it for fear an entire medical crew would rush in and run more tests. I went to my bedroom, activated the smooth ocean waves setting on my hover bed, and went to sleep as soon as I hit the warm gel mat, forgetting completely about the after party.

CHAPTER 14

FOOD OF
THE DOOMED

SLEEP WAS LIKE A WRESTLING MATCH. I was in and out of it with an army of dreams hunting me down. At one point I was a cyborg riding a dust worm through space, giant tendrils of shimmer-weave hair reaching toward me. I woke with a start. The room seemed unnaturally quiet. My hover sleeper was cold. The warm current no longer flowed through the gel pad beneath me. Several of the room systems were off.

"Jenson, lights at maximum," I said.

There was no answer. The room remained dark. My peripheral vision spotted a bloated figure lurking in the shadows at the corner of the room. My eyes locked onto my shiny, new DEMOTER X lying on the nightstand. Now that I was armed again, it only made sense to return to the old star pilot motto: 'Shoot first, check if they're still breathing, then shoot again just to be sure.'

I rolled off the hover sleeper, grabbing the DEMOTER in the process and landed in crouched position. The barrel of my pistol locked onto the bloated shape within the shadows.

I sent several blasts of energy into the darkness. The bright energy revealed the bloated shape to be a pile of silken pillows. A flurry of white feathers exploded outward and floated softly throughout the room.

"Bravo, Captain." A hissing voice said.

I spun toward the voice with the barrel of my weapon tracking along with my line of sight. There, at the foot of my hover sleeper stood Silvet. The snakelike creature was flanked by several dark wraiths.

"Remember, that gift was from me," Silvet motioned to the pistol. "If you shoot me, I may have to take it back."

I lowered the DEMOTER but my body remained tense. "Yes. Thank you. It saved my life earlier."

Silvet nodded. "So I hear. Apparently there are other forces that don't want you in this competition. No matter. We shall deal with them soon enough."

I nodded, not entirely clear what Silvet was talking about. Although I was grateful for the gift of the greatest energy pistol in the universe, I couldn't feel at ease as long as my room was filled with wraiths.

"So …" I searched for the words. "What are you doing here?"

"I wish to congratulate you on your success in the first competition. Parallax is quite pleased with your performance. He's decided to increase your incentive for victory."

A nervous shiver ran through my skin. I braced for the imminent threats generally associated with the word *incentive*. "How so?"

Silvet grinned. "If you succeed in the remaining competitions, Parallax will double your winnings."

My mind stuck for a moment. "Double? As in, two million vibes?"

"Correct."

It was hard enough to imagine having a million vibes. Two million was beyond my grasp. Pawn or not, I was feeling pretty lucky to be a part of this deal with Parallax.

"Just remember," Silvet said. "You are not to mention this to anyone." The wraiths floated throughout the room and appeared to melt into the shadows. "We are watching ... and listening."

I nodded, keeping a wary eye on every shadow in the room.

"And now, Captain." A circle of smoke began to rise around Silvet. "It is time for you to go back to sleep. Parallax wants his investment to be well rested. Farewell."

A great cloud of smoke filled the room. I coughed and waved the smoke from my face. After several moments, the smoke cleared and Silvet and the floating wraiths had disappeared. I laid back on the hover sleeper feeling overwhelmed. I'd had enough of this exhausting day that refused to end. I closed my eyes and soon entered a fitful sleep.

When I woke up, it seemed like I'd only slept a few trids. I sat up, squinting my bleary eyes in the dark room. Low harp music was playing, and a warm current was flowing through the gel pad on my hover sleeper.

"Jenson, what time is it?" My morning voice sounded like boots scraping over gravel.

A soft twinkling of bells preceded the computer's voice. "Good morning, sir. It's three marks past the helix rotation.

The competition starts in one trid, seven jemmins and three freems."

A memory flashed through my head of Silvet and my room filled with wraiths. "Jenson, after I went to sleep, did I have any ... visitors?"

"None on record, sir. Though, my systems had a short disturbance where monitoring was off for several jemmins. Most likely a system upgrade. Nothing to be troubled about."

I nodded, wondering if I'd dreamed the whole thing.

"Although there were a few destroyed pillows and quite a mess of feathers in your room after I came back online. A bit of late night target practice?"

I stiffened. So much for my dream theory. "Yeah, something like that."

"Sounds like rollicking good fun, sir."

It was hard to relax and begin the day knowing that I was being monitored. I tried to focus on the fact that this was a temporary situation, and I had a two million vibe payday waiting for me.

"Shall I begin the wake cycle?" Jenson said.

"Sure."

The sim curtains dissolved, letting the early Fantasmica sun fill the room. A cheerful classical tune replaced the harp sounds. I swung my legs out of bed and jumped to the floor. Instead of the cold metal shock of morning floor I was used to on my spaceship, my bare feet were greeted by the pre-warmed, velvety-soft, luxury carpeting.

"Sir, your sleep was quite restless," Jenson said. "Might I suggest the enhanced sleep chamber next time?"

A cylindrical, glass chamber just large enough for me to fit inside slid out from the wall.

"No way," I said. "That thing looks like a tomb. Someone gets control of this room again and I'll be trapped in there."

"Of course, sir. And again, allow me to express my deepest apologies for the loss of my technical controls. I assure you that—"

"Forget it." I didn't want him to start in on another stream of apologies. "Let's just get this day started."

"Certainly. Shall I prepare your morning meal?" Jenson said.

Holographic projections of gourmet platters appeared before me, artsy-looking arrangements of fruits and vegetables.

"What's this trash?" I said.

"These dishes are customized to your genetic composition to deliver optimal physical conditions for the competition."

"Blah, blah, blah. Get me some real food. Thick cuts of meat, gravy, fried stuff, you know."

"Of course, sir. But I must inform you that that type of consumption could inhibit your overall—"

"Don't care. Make it happen."

"Certainly. I apologize for my intrusive helpfulness."

New projections of gourmet meats, sauces and fried mystery clumps materialized and rotated slowly with aroma-enhanced technology that made my stomach all growly. I touched a few of the projections that looked like they had a nice layer of glaze on them. The projections lit up, then spun away.

"Excellent choices, sir." Jenson said. "A grand meal fit for a king."

"Yeah, well, the second challenge starts soon. This might just be my last meal."

"Insightful as well as poetic. Though I daresay after your stellar performance yesterday, no doubt you'll pull through with flying colors."

I was starting to like having Jenson around. I wondered what the cost would be for a computer personality transplant between him and Iris. I threw on my shirt and jacket, which slid over my new wings much easier now that I had the hang of things.

"Sir, your competitor entourage is waiting for you in the main area."

"Thanks Jenson." I pulled on my boots and walked into the main area of my room.

Blix and Nelvan were sitting on silken pillows with their heads bowed and eyes closed.

"And Lord," Nelvan said. "Please help the captain retain all his limbs in today's challenge and not grow any more creepy wings or anything."

I gave a loud clearing of my throat.

"Amen." Blix smiled and stood. "Good morning, Captain."

"That the best prayer you got?" I gave them a questioning look. "I mean, if you're gonna seek divine help, ask for my resounding victory and for my competitors to get crushed under rocks or something."

"Well, you missed the beginning of our prayer." Blix motioned to Nelvan as if seeking affirmation. "It was very much like that."

"Yeah," Nelvan nodded. "Except not as mean toward the other players."

Nelvan stood and I noticed he wore a brown kandrelian hide jacket.

"What's with the jacket?" I said.

"You like it?" Nelvan straightened the jacket and squared his shoulders.

I nodded. "Yeah, not bad."

"It's horrid." Blix eyed Nelvan like a disappointed parent. "And to think, just last night Nelvan won the fashion award at the after party. His old earth jumpsuit was the talk of the Glittronium fashion council."

Nelvan wore a bashful smile. "Crazy, huh? I didn't even shower yesterday."

"The award was a Sellisan silk blazer with fine crimson stitching." Blix looked upward as if catching a glimpse of heaven. "I turn my back for a moment and he's traded his glorious blazer for that ... thing." Blix pointed at the jacket as if it were a monster.

Nelvan shrugged. "The blazer was weird. Some guy offered me this great jacket for it."

"If I ever find that charlatan ..." Blix clenched his fist.

I moved toward Nelvan and put an arm over his shoulder. "Whattya think Blix?" I motioned from the boy to me. "The Captain and his junior star explorer."

Blix shook his head. "If Nelvan is going to emulate anyone, it should be someone with some fashion sense."

"Don't listen to him, Nelvan." I patted him on the back. "You never looked better."

Nelvan beamed with pride. "Thanks, Captain."

I took a quick look around the room. "Where's Jasette?"

Blix gave me a sympathetic look. "Relationship troubles?"

"No. I mean ... none of your business," I said. "Have you seen her?"

Blix looked away. "I can't say."

I let out an exasperated grunt. "Nelvan?"

Nelvan shot a nervous look to Blix. "Um, I think she's eating with ... someone."

My teeth involuntarily ground together. "Forglyn. He conned her into some fancy, romantic breakfast so he could steal her away."

Nelvan gave a sad little nod. I gripped the handle of my shiny, new DEMOTER X and looked toward the windowed wall of my room. The industrious maintenance robots had already replaced it with a clean, clear panel of thick glass. I fantasized about blasting Forglyn through the glass the same way I'd dispatched that filthy cyborg.

"Sir," Jenson said. "Your meal is ready."

My glorious plates of battered and glazed food emerged from the large, ivory table near the window. I strode over and immediately started in on a thick cut of meat with a beautiful coating of grease. It was moist and full of savory deliciousness. This place definitely wasn't skimping on the quality of the food. It almost made up for their lack of security.

Blix and Nelvan joined me at the table.

"Ugh, Captain." Blix cast a repulsed look at the food. "This is hardly competition-level fare."

"Who cares?" I grabbed a battered stick of cheese and took a big bite. "It tastes great." I spoke with a mouth full of food in hopes of silencing him.

"He's got a point, Blix." Nelvan was sampling a fried, moon-shaped meat. He dipped it in a rich-looking sauce and took a bite. The sauce dribbled down his chin as he gave me a hearty nod. "It's pretty tasty."

I cast a victorious grin at Blix. "By the way, Nelvan, keep your lie detecting abilities ready. I want to know who I can trust around here."

"I'll try, Captain." Nelvan frowned. "But to be honest, ever since we got here, it seems like most everyone is lying. It even feels like you're holding something back from us."

I let out a nervous cough. "Me? Come on."

Blix narrowed his eyes. "Are you, Captain?"

"Of course not. Don't be stupid." I took a big bite to avoid further conversation.

Blix gave me a look like he wasn't convinced and sat on a plush pillow nearby. "Let's move on to other things."

"Great." I grabbed a cup of rich broth and took a deep swig.

"Captain," Blix said. "Before you enter the next challenge, I suggest you reconcile your issues with Jasette."

"I tried." I held up grease-covered hands in resignation. "She won't return my communicator signals."

Blix frowned. "That's hardly effort, Captain. I heard about your little escapade with Selinxia. You need to seek her out and give a sincere apology."

I pounded a fist on the table, sending a plate of buttery rolls flying. "Nothing happened. We were just talking."

Nelvan shot a scrutinizing look my way. "I dunno, Captain. I was watching Behind the Scenes of the Iron Gauntlet this morning, and they said you were flexing for her with your shirt off."

I pointed a forkful of meat at him. "That's a lie.... Okay, fine, I had my shirt off but I never flexed. I have a naturally bulky build."

Nelvan shared an unconvinced look with Blix. "Well, the actor that was portraying you in the re-enactment clip was really putting on a show for her. Sparks were flying."

I stood and threw a platter of sauce at the wall. It shattered into several white shards and painted a greasy waterfall over the wall mural. "Those filthy skrids! That's not what happened at all."

"Captain." Blix frowned. "Please control yourself. Stretching the truth for dramatic theater is what Glittronium is built on. You wanted to be on the show. You'd better get used to it and stop leaving a mess for others to clean." He motioned to the greasy wall.

"Don't worry, sir." Jenson chimed in. "I'll have this cleaned upon your return. It's good to express your feelings now and again. Good show, I say."

I looked at Blix and motioned to the ceiling. "There, you see? Jenson gets me. Supportive and encouraging in my time of need. You should take notes."

Blix sighed. "It's your luxury room service computer. Civil as Jenson is, his bolstering of your bad behavior is only enabling a slide toward immaturity." Blix looked toward the ceiling. "No offense, Jenson."

"None taken, sir," Jenson spoke cheerfully. "It was an astute observation."

Blix raised his eyebrows. "I rest my case."

I had no intention of admitting Blix was right. Instead, I grabbed a thick rib coated with spices and stood. "Come on. I've got a good helping of rage built up for today's challenge." I took a huge bite of the rib and led the way out of the room.

CHAPTER 15

THE MOON
CHALLENGE

THE TRANSVERSE CUBE rushed us to the first floor of Shansmannor Hall. It was not kind to the greasy meats and sauces sloshing around in my stomach. Several unwholesome sounds gurgled. If 444 flights of stairs weren't so daunting, I would've walked.

In the crystalline foyer, security forces were everywhere. Guests filed through scanning orbs and sensor wand sweeps. I was impressed that my ambush had given rise to such precautions.

"Look at this," I leaned back and crossed my arms, basking in the sight. "It's nice to see they're taking competitor safety seriously."

"It's not that, Captain," Blix said. "The Iron Gauntlet prize vault was compromised last night. Didn't you hear?"

My ego took a hit of humility. "Oh. What happened?"

"From what I hear, someone disabled two layers of code barriers and took out ten Impaler Drones before tripping the alarm and escaping."

"What's an Impaler Drone?" Nelvan said.

Blix made a disgusted expression. "You don't want to know."

"Well, if it increases the security around here, I'm all for it," I said.

After several rounds of scans and security wand prodding I could have done without, we were cleared to enter the main room. When we got there, it was already filled with Iron Gauntlet fans. The sim visuals of the expansive room placed the crowd on the charred surface of a volcanic planet. Bright orange lava flows created deep troughs on the blackened landscape. These became visual walkways for the fans that wandered the room sipping their drinks and socializing.

Towering volcanoes erupted in the distance spewing brilliant orange showers into the sky.

"These simulators are fantastic." Blix had his hands on his hips, swiveling back and forth in admiration of the room. "Glittronium sure knows how to put on a show."

"I liked yesterday's better." Nelvan cringed. "This reminds me of that creepy moon with all those space monkeys."

A shiver went through me at the monkey memory. "Don't remind me of those vile creatures."

"Glint." Forglyn waved from a nearby lava flow. "Over here."

I frowned. "Speaking of vile creatures."

Jasette stood next to Forglyn, the orange glow of the lava lighting their faces like a bonfire.

Blix nudged me. "Now's your chance. Go make things right before the challenge begins."

I marched over to Forglyn with Blix and Nelvan at my heels.

"Welcome back, Glint." Forglyn was decked out in a

shimmering, golden suit. His dark hair was so uniformly styled, it seemed if a single strand dared move out of place, it would die instantly.

I grabbed the handle of my DEMOTER X in case I felt like escalating things. Jasette had her arms crossed and her expression was stoic. My mind wavered between an apology or unfounded accusations about her shared breakfast with Forglyn. All my grown up emotions told me to put petty, jealous impulses aside and play it classy. "So, how was your stupid, little breakfast? Lots of kissy-kissy?"

Jasette looked at me like she was confused and disgusted simultaneously.

Forglyn chuckled. "Just old friends catching up. I was a perfect gentleman."

I stared him down. "Sure you were."

Blix cleared his throat. "Captain, wasn't there something you wanted to say to Jasette?"

Jasette gave a half-hearted look as if whatever I had to say would be promptly swatted down and crushed beneath her heel.

I squared my jaw. "Nope."

We stared each other down for a few moments of silence. Suddenly, I realized a small cambot was circling us.

Forglyn moved between us, well aware of the cambot. The glowing audio sphere hovered in front of his mouth. "Tensions are high in the Iron Gauntlet today. As you can see, the drama doesn't end at the challenges."

Before I could launch into an angry response, a bright hoverdisc lit up underneath Forglyn and raised him high overhead.

"Welcome, one and all," Forglyn's amplified voice boomed

throughout the room, "to the second challenge of the Iron Gauntlet!"

The crowd erupted in hoots and cheers. The thunderous stomping of the death march filled the room.

"Please welcome our surviving contestants. Chessandrillia, Chakdragonnon, Dentrylich, and Glint Starcrost."

The crowd broke into applause. A bright pedestal lit up underneath me, and I was lifted upward. Pedestals lit up and raised the other contestants simultaneously.

"And what challenge would be complete without an Iron Gauntlet surprise twist?"

A huge volcano erupted behind Forglyn, the bright orange casting him in dark silhouette. He raised his hands and glowing competitor bracelets shone brightly on his wrists. As if in response, all the bracelets worn by competitors and their entourages lit up.

"Today's twist will project a holographic presence of the competitors' entourages to aid them in the challenge. And they'll need all the help they can get to survive ... Dr. Visikuller's moon of a million rooms!"

A rumble of low oohs went through the crowd.

The bright shock of teleportation energy shot up from my pedestal and froze me in place. As my molecules drifted away, I thought of all the space bar horror stories I'd heard about that moon.

CHAPTER 16

THE MOON OF
A MILLION ROOMS

ONCE THE SHOCK of the teleportation wore off, I found myself in a small, brightly lit room. The walls, ceiling, and floor were spotless. A white glow seemed to emanate from the walls, providing the illumination. There were no furnishings of any kind.

The walls were bare except for a plain shelf with three levers on the far wall. All in all, it wasn't as bad as I expected.

Zero sound came from my bracelet. Apparently the connection was severed. Forglyn's surprise announcement that my crew would join me in holographic form had given me a bit of hope. But now that the bracelet connection was lost, my guess was that the holograms were experiencing the same technical glitch. Once again, technology was sticking it to me.

I waited in silence, wondering if some impending horror was going to join me in the room. After several moments of quiet boredom, I started to question the tall tales I'd heard about this place. An unending labyrinth of mysterious chambers, danger at every step, hideous creatures of forgotten planets trapped within, no escape, blah, blah, blah.

I always figured it was trumped up ghost stories and now that I was in this nice, clean room, it only confirmed my suspicions.

I raised the bracelet to my ear for any trace of a connection. Silence. I was on my own.

I took a few moments to examine the walls and floor. There were no doors or seams of any kind. Even the ceiling, although slightly out of reach, didn't show the slightest hairline crack on its perfectly smooth surface.

My attention drifted back to the three levers on the simple, white shelf. The levers sat there, taunting me. They dared me to approach and activate some unknown terror.

Since it was just a matter of time and I hate waiting, I decided to face the inevitable. I approached the levers carefully, fingering the handle of the DEMOTER X in case of sudden attacks. The levers were a plain, white color like everything else in the room, without markings of any kind. All three were a similar obelisk shape, but upon closer inspection I noticed slight variations.

The first lever had a curve on the back. The second was perfectly straight on every side. The third was a little shorter than the others. If these subtle differences held any clues about what lever to activate, it was thoroughly lost on me. If they all looked exactly the same; it was still a random roll of the dice.

Since there wasn't much to go on, I decided to follow the first random theories that popped into my head. Experience had taught me it's a bad idea to trust the first option in a sketchy place. So, the first lever was out. Also, the third option is usually just an add-on used to increase the complexity of the choice and therefore, by design, would be the wrong pick.

The more I thought about it, the middle lever was the clear choice. Even the shape was the most sound. No deviant curves or diminished height to announce its obvious inferiority.

As I grabbed the middle lever, I was feeling pretty good about my powers of deduction. The lever was cool to the touch—cool and collected, just like my impressive analytical skills. Pulling the lever produced a small clicking sound. I drew the DEMOTER and took a few steps back, waiting for the results of my choice.

The room was silent for several long moments. There were no sounds except the invigorating hum of energy coming from my pistol.

I started to wonder if I should pull another one.

Suddenly, a burst of applause came from my bracelet that set my heart racing. The holographic forms of my crew materialized around me. They were all slightly translucent with a soft, blue glow. Blix and Nelvan swiveled around as if trying to find some lurking space creature. Jasette had a studied expression as she looked about.

"My apologies to the Iron Gauntlet viewers," Forglyn's voice sounded thin as it came from the bracelet. "Temporary disturbance. Deep space transmission can be such a pain." A smattering of polite laughter came from the crowd.

"Captain." Blix's hologram moved toward me. "Are you okay? We lost you for a bit."

"He looks pale ... and kind of slouchy." Nelvan's face was filled with concern. "What happened, Captain?"

I glared at Nelvan. "Nothing, I'm fine. I just can't find a way out of here."

"Avoid impulsive actions." Jasette moved closer to the

wall, giving it a close examination. "Escaping these rooms is a methodical process."

Blix looked at the levers. He turned to me, his face serious. "You didn't touch any of those levers, did you?"

I paused for a moment. "No."

Blix frowned. "Captain?"

"Okay, I touched the middle one."

"What?" Blix was wide eyed. "That's the worst one."

Jasette shook her head. "Typical."

"Relax." I felt myself getting very non-relaxed. "Nothing happened."

A section of the floor slid away with a soft whooshing sound. A dark hole was left in its place.

"Uh-oh."

Blix rushed to the levers. "You started an unlocking sequence." He leaned in to examine them. "You must finish the sequence before the system completes a counter response."

I hurried over. "Okay, which one do I pull?"

"No, no pulling. These are engineered for subtle shift variance codes." Blix paused, looking up at me. "Wait, you didn't pull the lever, did you?"

"Maybe."

Blix buried his head in his hands. A large section of the floor next to me whooshed away.

"Okay, here's what we need to do ..." Blix studied the levers with nervous energy.

"Captain," Nelvan said. "Why don't you just—"

"Not now, Nelvan," I said.

"Okay, here's the sequence," Blix said. "One, half turn. Three, touch, touch, full turn. One, reverse turn, touch.

Two, light touch. Three, full turn, light touch, touch. Then repeat the sequence but in reverse order. Got it?"

"No, I don't *got it*." I glared at him. "I don't even understand what you said. Is 'one' the first lever?"

He let loose an angry hiss. "Of course it's the first lever. Now do a half turn, then touch the third lever twice before giving it a full turn."

"You know, you could always just—" Nelvan started.

"Not now, boy." I gave the first lever a half turn and a loud clunking noise sounded.

"No, to the right!" Blix yelled. "Why did you turn it to the left?"

"You didn't say which way to turn it!"

"It's common knowledge!"

At that moment, the floor beneath my feet slid away and I fell into the darkness.

THE MOON
LABYRINTH

THE TERROR OF MY FREEFALL lasted only freems. Soon I was sliding against a smooth metal wall constructed on a gradual slope. I scrambled at the slope in a panic, searching for a handhold. Sounds echoed around me, giving the sense that I was in a tunnel. A blue flicker of light was visible ahead. I sped toward the light at terrifying speed. I swallowed hard, my mind racing through the possible landings of spikes, fire and awaiting pools of acid.

The tunnel came to an abrupt end. I was launched into huge, grey cavern, stalactites covering the ceiling, and I hurtled toward a sluggish, green river that wound through the cavern. Right before I hit the water, I remembered my wings.

The water stung my skin on impact. My nose filled with a thick, repulsive slime. As I plunged into the murky depths, I thought of how obvious and logical it would've been to simply fly and avoid my watery predicament. Curse my fickle short-term memory. I struggled to get my bearings in a river filled with ropey strands of slimy river vegetation that seemed eager to take hold of me. I finally broke through the surface, gasping for air and spitting out bits of slime.

The current was sluggish, and I made quick progress toward the riverbank. A few feet from the edge, something very large and slimy nudged my leg, and the sudden fear of some lurking water creature made me swim like a madman. I reached the cold stone of the cavern floor and scrambled to get away from the river's edge. Without looking back to see whatever dark, hideous shape loomed behind me, I sprinted toward a thick cluster of stalagmites and took cover.

I drew my DEMOTER and peeked out. The river flowed along, providing cover for whatever vile beast swam its depths. I stood there dripping and breathing heavily for several moments, but there were no signs of a creature. After a few quiet moments with nothing but the lonely dripping of the cavern stalactites, my heart rate slowed from panic rhythm.

It seemed safe for the moment, but I was keeping my distance from that river. Whatever was in there felt big and dangerous. If it had any grasping tentacles or land-crawling abilities, I wanted to be far, far away.

I slunk back behind the stalagmite cluster and took a quick look around. The cavern was large and filled with creepy echoes. A soft, phosphorescent glow provided subtle illumination and promised to cast a ghostly gleam on any creatures waiting to jump out and bite me. There was nothing left to do but venture through the cavern and look for a way out. But the moment I took a step forward, there was movement behind the next closest grouping of stalagmites. I aimed my weapon in the direction of the sounds.

"Who's there?" I called out in the gruffest voice I could muster.

The bulky figure that stepped out from the stalagmites sent fear tremors down my spine—it was none other than the evil cyborg that broke into my room back at Glittronium. How was he still alive? And how in blazes did he get here?

"Gleeeent Steeercrost." His broken, metallic voice called out to me. "Tiiime to coooollect."

He trudged toward me. His metal chest piece was blackened and pitted. Obviously my gun had left its mark but the fact that he was still alive and kicking meant he was no typical cyborg.

I decided to make his demise a little more certain this time. As I leveled my gun toward him, it was yanked free from my hand. It flew toward the cyborg and stopped in front of his open hand. A pulsating, electrical current appeared to be holding it in place.

"Not theeese tiiime Gleeeent." He hurled the gun deep into the cavern. I winced at the sound of it skipping across the rocky ground in the distance.

"Who are you?" I demanded. "How did you get here?" I tried to casually move around the stalagmite cluster for a clear exit.

"Mar Mar's priiiize." He pointed his thick, metallic finger at me. "I have come to coooollect."

A metallic cable shot out from his palm but I was ready. I dove out of the way. The cable just missed and deflected off the stalagmite behind me. I rolled to my feet and sprinted toward the green river.

The memory of the water creature brought me to a dead stop. I tried to change course. It was a costly mistake. The metal cable snaked around my ankle and constricted. A strong pull took my feet out from under me and sent me to the unforgiving ground in a rush. The fall took the wind out of me and I lay there, gasping for air.

"I taaake yoooou to Mar Mar." The hollow voice of the cyborg gained in intensity as it pulled me closer.

I clawed at the ground, looking for anything that remotely resembled a weapon. As he pulled me within reach, I grabbed a handful of dust and pebbles. He leaned over, grasped my jacket with one hand and lifted me in the air. Suddenly, I was face to face with the metal monstrosity. The red band of light that passed for his eyes glowed brightly. I threw my handful of pebbles at his face. They bounced off with soft, clinking sounds. He didn't even flinch. A repeating, grating sound came from the grid of holes that acted as his mouth. I could only assume it was a cyborg version of laughter.

His rocket boots ignited in a flare of orange. He lifted me off the ground and a wave of fear swept through me. I struggled to free myself from his vice-like grip but it wouldn't budge.

He flew forward with a lurch, carrying me through the air like a bird with fresh prey.

I remembered my wings this time and flapped wildly to help break free. His grip held firm, my efforts only serving to twist my jacket around his metal hand.

As we flew over the green river, I caught a glimpse of a large, shadowy form moving through the water. It appeared to be following us. I gave my full attention to the river in time to see a giant, green sea serpent leaping from the water. His fang filled mouth was opened wide to receive us.

CHAPTER 18

THE DEATH BOX

THE RIVER SERPENT launched toward us. The cyborg weaved to the side to avoid the oncoming jaws of death. Having glimpsed the creature in advance, I was a step ahead of my captor, and in his momentary confusion, his grip on my jacket relaxed. With a strong flap of wings, I broke free and dove away.

I barely avoided the hungry mouth of the river beast. His luminous, green eye followed after me as I glided alongside his body. Thankfully, my captor wasn't as lucky—a quick glance backward offered a wonderfully gruesome sight. His metal body disappeared as the serpent's mouth engulfed him. The beast dove back to the river, carrying the cyborg to his watery grave with a terrific splash.

My lungs burned as I gasped for air. Apparently I'd held my breath for the entire horrific experience. I flew clear of the river, keeping as high as possible to avoid any further cavern creatures but not so high as to be reverse impaled on the pointy stalactites. One thing was certain—I didn't want to go any further without a weapon. I circled above the area where it seemed the cyborg had thrown my pistol. The stark, grey contrast of the cavern floor offered some help, and soon the lustrous metal of the DEMOTER winked at me like an old friend.

After retrieving my weapon, I took to the air again. I wanted to avoid any shadowy unknowns lurking within the stalagmites.

The presence of that cyborg down here threw me for a loop. Discovering that he was some kind of deranged bounty hunter trying to bring me back to Mar Mar the Unthinkable answered a few of the whys, but how did he get down here? It made no sense. Plus, now that he was dead, it was going to remain a bizarre and unsolved mystery. Whatever the explanation, it didn't matter if I remained stuck in this cavern. For the time being, I had to focus on finding a way out.

I continued down the expansive cavern, staying well clear of the green river, looking for any tunnel that might lead to freedom. Everything started to look the same. A never-ending series of grey rock cavern littered with stalactites and stalagmites. It felt like I was flying through a large torture device about to clamp down at any moment.

After a while, my wings grew fatigued. I considered switching back to walking. The cavern was getting increasingly narrow, and I'd been forced to fly uncomfortably close to the river.

There didn't appear to be any caves or overhead passages that promised a way out. My guess was that I missed something along the way and needed to double back. Plus, this part of the cavern was making me claustrophobic. Just as I decided to head back, I spied what looked like a door in the wall of the cavern. High stalagmites rose up on either side of it, making me wonder if I would have missed it had I been on foot.

I landed right in front of it. The stone door was obviously fashioned by some intelligent being, with a handle in the middle. I examined it for a moment, Blix's voice still ringing in my head about not touching anything. It looked like a plain door to me, and since my bracelet connection was broken again, I had to take matters into my own hands.

The handle was a half-circle shape that protruded just enough for a handhold. I gave it a half turn to the right to avoid a future 'I told you so' from Blix.

There was a series of metal clicks, and the door slid open with the teeth-clenching sound of stone grating upon stone. Beyond was a wood paneled room about half the size of the bridge on my star freighter.

A scraping sound came from overhead. I looked up to find a detached stalactite plunging toward me. My muscles tensed, I dove into the room ahead, and the pointed stone crashed to the ground in a cloud of dust and rubble.

A pile of stone now lay where I'd stood only freems ago. A fleeting thought about how lucky I was evaporated when the door of the room closed behind me.

I drew my pistol and checked my surroundings. The floor was constructed from marbled glowstone. It appeared to be one of the weaker variations as the illumination was low. The wood paneled room was empty except for a plain, wooden table and chair against the far wall. Beside the table lay a long, wooden box the size of my sleeping slab.

A series of static crackles came from my bracelet, and in a quick flash of blue light my holographic crew stood around me once more.

Blix took quick glances around the room. "Where are you?"

"No idea," I said. "Where have you been?"

"Cosmic interference." Jasette said matter-of-factly.

"We were quite worried, Captain," Blix said. "Even my thought messages couldn't seem to break through."

I pointed a threatening finger. "I told you, no thoughting."

Blix narrowed his eyes.

"What happened to your jacket?" Nelvan pointed toward my chest.

I examined the lapels of my kandrelian hide jacket, noticing a few new rips. "That filthy skrid ripped my jacket."

"Who?" said Blix.

"That cyborg," I said. "The same one that ambushed my room."

Blix gave me a confused look. "You're referring to the one who fell 444 floors, correct?"

"Yeah."

Blix shared an amused look with Jasette. "Captain, as unlikely as it is that he survived such a fall, an even more improbable event would be for the same cyborg to be on that moon with you."

I raised my hands in bewilderment. "Well, that's what happened."

Blix rubbed his chin. "You feeling alright? Have there been other hallucinations?"

"It wasn't a hallucination," I glared at him. "He was here. He's a bounty hunter for Mar Mar."

"It's okay, Glint." Jasette gave me a concerned look. "Just calm down. Do you see the cyborg in the room with us now?"

"Of course not," I said. "He got eaten by a river serpent."

"Yes, of course." Blix nodded and motioned to the others as if they were supposed to agree. "We all see the cyborg and the river serpent now, clear as day. Now let's just lie down and take a short nap, shall we?"

"Would you shut up," I said. "I'm not imagining things. Nelvan, you believe me, right?"

Nelvan gave a weak smile. "Um ..."

"Forget it. By the way, what were you trying to tell me before?"

"Oh yeah," Nelvan said. "The floor was falling, and I was going to mention you can fly now. Did you remember?"

I made a mental note to listen closer to the boy next time. "Yeah, of course."

Jasette walked around the room, taking a closer look at the simple furnishings. "Did you touch anything yet?"

I frowned. "No. I just got here."

Blix took a cursory look around. "The simpler the room, the more complex the solution. This could take some time."

"Thanks, that's zero help." I turned to Jasette and Nelvan. "Any ideas?"

Jasette pointed to the long wooden box. "If I were you, I wouldn't touch that thing."

I nodded in agreement. It was far too close to a coffin to mess with.

"Maybe you could check the table," Nelvan said. "If someone wrote on it, there might be impressions in the wood."

Blix gave me a hopeful look and soon we were both at the table. I grabbed my communicator and expanded it to a large, translucent blue rectangle.

I initiated the analytics, and several thin rays of blue light shone onto the table. The light rays traced frenzied patterns on the wood.

A grid of results appeared in small icons on the screen. I hit the first one and a few lines of script emerged.

Day 23. I have avoided the death box at all costs, but my supplies have run out. I see no other way out. If it provides escape, I will continue this message.

I gave a wary glance at the long wooden box beside me. The fact that a previous visitor called it the 'death box' was enough to tweak my stomach when I looked at it.

The next icon on my communicator produced a visual of indecipherable charts.

I turned to Blix. "This mean anything to you?"

Blix studied the charts. "Strange. It starts as a systematic analysis of this room. The logic was quite sound at first but it gradually breaks down into the scribbles of a lunatic."

"Well, that's comforting." I tried several additional icons that offered no help. Some were desperate last words, others were logs of failed escapes. Finally, there was one icon left.

The last icon produced a short message.

Greetings, traveler. I am Dr. Visikuller. If you've deciphered this writing, then you've solved the riddle of the room. The solution is quite simple. Pry open the wooden container beside you. That is all. Have a nice day.

I turned to my crew. "Whattya think?"

Jasette shook her head. "Don't touch it."

"I don't get it," Nelvan said. "Why would he leave that note?"

"Dr. Visikuller was mad," Blix said. "He spent most of his life and vast fortune building this labyrinth of insanity. His words are not to be trusted."

A defeated feeling made my bones feel heavy. "Well, I guess I'll keep looking."

"Yes," Blix said. "And see if you can prompt that *temper* of yours into action."

I gave him a dark look and set to a careful examination of the room. After a few trids of searching every inch of the room and finding no openings, latches, or vulnerabilities of any kind, I was out of patience. "I give up. That box is the only thing left to try."

Blix looked up from the corner of the room he was studying. "Captain, that's exactly what the mad doctor wants."

"I'm tired of looking. If that skrid didn't leave a key, the box is the only chance."

"Wait." Jasette's face brightened. "That's it. Maybe he did leave a key."

"I looked everywhere," I said. "No keys."

"Maybe these are the key." She motioned to the furniture. "Fit them together the right way and who knows?"

Blix nodded. "Definitely worth a try."

I'd tried everything else. At this point, it was the best idea I'd heard.

"Try it, Captain." Nelvan beamed.

I tried a few stacking configurations using the table and chair. Jasette suggested stacking them on the box, which I was not excited about. I set to work taking great care not to accidentally knock the lid off the box and unleash whatever evils lay in wait.

Upon closer inspection, I noticed the box lightly tapered in where it met the wall. I lifted the chair against the wall and lowered it on the box. The legs fit snuggly on either side. As it slid to the floor, a small click sounded.

"Ha!" Jasette smiled. "I was right."

"Now the table, Captain." Blix was pushing at the table with holographic hands as if that would help.

I flipped the table upside down and laid it on top of the box. I slid it carefully forward until it met the chair. It perfectly covered the remaining surface. There was another click and the sound of large machinery in motion came from the wall at my right. With a heavy, grinding sound, the wall slid away revealing a darkened room beyond.

"It worked." Nelvan clapped.

"Brilliant, your majesty." Blix bowed to Jasette. "Captain, don't you want to say something to Jasette?"

Normally Blix's prodding only made my heels dig in further, but I was so relieved to be free of that small, dark room I didn't care anymore.

I turned to Jasette's hologram. "Great call on the room key. Thanks. And hey, I'm sorry about last night."

"And what about this morning?"

"Right, that too."

Her expression was still guarded but she softened a bit. "We'll talk about it when you get back. Just make sure you get out of here before the door closes."

I nodded and hurried into the next room. My feet made crunching noises as I entered the dark room, and there was a rumbling thud as the door closed behind me.

A single overhead light clicked on, illuminating a stone-walled room. The floor was comprised of tiny black pebbles, which accounted for the crunching sounds. A sleek-looking, silver, two-seater space cruiser was the focal point of an otherwise empty space. The light shone directly on it, and the smooth lines of the cruiser were calling out to me. I'd never seen a craft quite like it. It looked fast and agile and ready to fly me off this crummy little moon.

"An obvious trap," Blix said.

I ignored him, admiring the shiny silver hull of the spaceship.

"Glint?" Jasette was watching me with concern. "You're not thinking of going near that thing, are you?"

I threw up my hands. "What am I supposed to do? There's nothing else in here." I motioned to the blank stone walls.

"But where would you fly it?" Nelvan said.

The boy had a point. The walls and ceiling were solid stone except for the orb shaped light overhead.

"Unlocking these rooms demands intense scrutiny," Blix said. "The solution could hardly be as obvious as that spaceship."

"Fine," I said. "I'll examine the room."

I took a few steps forward and suddenly my foot sank into the pebbles. I fell to my hands and knees as the floor gave way. The surrounding pebbles poured in as I sank further. I twisted and fell to my side. The pebbles started to give way beneath my weight. This time I remembered my wings. Several hard flaps sent a spray of black pebbles around the room. My heart leapt as I started to pull free.

"Captain, look out!" Nelvan cried.

Dark tentacles as thick as my arm emerged from the pebbles nearby. They groped around as if searching for something. Since that something was me, I flapped much harder. My foot broke free just as a tentacle lunged toward me and wrapped around my thigh.

The black tentacle held firm and I couldn't take flight, even with my fear-induced flapping. Two more tentacles shot toward me and wrapped around my arms. I struggled to reach my DEMOTER but it was no use—my arms were held fast. The tentacles pulled me toward the pebbles with a strength that made me deathly afraid of the monstrosity they belonged to.

Three more tentacles broke forth from the pebbles, wrapping around my legs. I felt a surge of panic as they pulled me down. A small part of my consciousness was aware that my crew was shouting advice at me. But however helpful it was, my fear had reached a point where it all sounded like gibberish.

CHAPTER 19

TENTACLES
AND TUNNELS

THE TENTACLES SLAMMED me into the pebbles and I started to sink. In a last burst of strength I twisted my body and grasped one of the tentacles with both hands, my fingers digging into it as if I were strangling my worst enemy. A prickling sensation went through my hands as though I'd grabbed a quill-covered moon rat, and the tentacle in my hands writhed like a snake trying to escape. A rumble went through the pebbles beneath me.

I felt a renewed strength in my hands. I gripped harder and a muffled shriek came from the pebbles. The tentacles released their hold on me and slithered back into the ground. I let go of the one still in my hands and it rushed away like some terrified serpent.

I sat up, breathing heavily and scanning the area for any remaining tentacles. For the moment, the pebbles had stopped sinking. I breathed deeply and wiped the panic sweat from my forehead. That's when I noticed my hands—hands that no longer resembled my human hands. I lifted them toward my face and turned them over slowly, not believing what I saw—thick orange scales that ended in sharp claws where my normal nails used to be. I stared in silent horror at the sight.

"Amazing," Blix said. "Captain, that is a fortunate turn indeed."

I looked at him in shock. A violent rumble went through the pebbles and the floor swayed, so I took flight immediately, not wanting a second attack catching me off guard. Coming to terms with my freaky new lizard hands would have to wait. My only thought at the moment was survival.

Despite the warnings of my crew, there was only one path to take. I flew like a laser blast straight for the cockpit of the spaceship. Tentacles sprang from the pebbles below. They twisted and writhed through the room seeking revenge.

I didn't want to get caught without my weapon this time. I drew the DEMOTER and held it at the ready as I flew under an extended black tentacle that swatted the air and landed on top of the spaceship.

The cockpit opened with a few simple clasp locks and I jumped inside. Two tentacles reached toward me. A few glorious DEMOTER blasts sent them writhing away. The spaceship trembled and swayed. Whatever lay beneath the pebbles was getting very angry.

I slammed the cockpit shut and scanned the control panel. It was an older craft, utilizing a series of outdated dials and knobs arranged in unorthodox patterns. I'd flown enough ships to find my way around unusual control panels, but I still needed a moment to soak it all in.

My holographic crew appeared on the passenger seat. All three of them were stacked together in the same space, which made for a very odd visual.

"I can't believe you went for the ship," Blix said. "After I expressly warned—"

"Shut up!" I hit a few switches that lit up the controls and fired up the engine.

A tentacle slammed against the cockpit.

"Get this thing moving," Jasette said.

"Give me a freem." I turned a few dials and the ship started to power back down.

Several dark tentacles sprang up and began wrapping around the ship.

"Hurry, Captain!" Nelvan said.

My fingers trembled as they activated a few more knobs and the ship roared back to life. The engines powered to full and hovered off the pebbled ground. I was starting to get a sense of the ship controls. A large section of the stone wall in front of the ship slid away, revealing a dimly lit tunnel.

"Ha!" I turned to Blix. "The ship was a big mistake, huh? It must've been on a pressure plate. Lift off and bam! An exit tunnel opens right up."

Blix huffed a laugh. "A tunnel to where?"

"Anywhere but here." I grabbed the two-handed steering mechanism and edged it forward. The craft moved slightly, then swayed from side to side as it struggled to break free of the tentacles. A shudder went through the spaceship, and the engines whined with the effort.

"What's that?" Nelvan pointed his shaking, holographic hand toward the side of the cockpit. A towering shape rose up from the pebbles. It was the hideous, one-eyed owner of the grasping tentacles. The focal point of his dark, sloping head was a gaping mouth with several rows of sharp-looking teeth. He opened his mouth wide and a trumpet-like roar filled the room.

"I'm glad I'm a hologram," Nelvan said.

I gave him a dark look but couldn't help being envious.

"Focus!" Jasette said. "You need to do something fast."

My eyes danced across the controls until I found the right switch. "Okay, let's see what kind of firepower this thing has."

I hit the controls and a spray of red beams tore into the tentacles wrapped around the nose of the ship. A hideous shriek filled the room and the tentacles receded.

My body leaned as I pushed the throttle forward. The ship rocketed into the tunnel. I let loose a shout of victory as the creature's trumpeting howl faded into the distance.

The smooth, finished walls of the tunnel soon gave way to a narrow cavern. I'd located the exterior lights to keep from smashing into the grey walls of the winding passage. The circular cavern seemed as though it was fashioned by some giant moon worm. I tried not to think about running into a worm of that size as I checked the walls for alternate passages.

"There's something up there." Jasette motioned ahead.

A yellow glow illuminated the end of the cavern. I brought the ship to a crawl as we hovered into a vast, underground space. Small flecks of luminous yellow brought a soft light to the expansive area. The sense of being very small came over me. I turned the nose of the ship in all directions as we inched forward, trying to get a sense of things.

The ceiling and floor stretched into an unseen darkness. A myriad of other tunnel-like caverns broke off in an endless choice of paths.

"One of these tunnels better lead out of here," I said.

"How can you know which one?" Nelvan said.

"I believe that's the intent," Blix said. "A classic Vrexollian dilemma. An array of choices so daunting it becomes no choice at all."

"Nonsense," Jasette said. "You just have to choose smart. Any nav guidance controls on this ship?"

"No," I said. "I've already checked."

"Well, you have eight more trids in the day," Blix said. "As long as you find an Iron Gauntlet necklace to transport you back to Glittronium, you won't be stuck on this moon for the rest of your life."

"Remind me to blast you when I get back." I swerved the ship into a nearby tunnel. For some reason, I had a really good feeling about it.

"Wait, why are you choosing this one?" Jasette said.

"I'm going with my gut. Don't worry, my instincts haven't failed me yet."

About eight trids later, I was flying the ship down yet another tunnel that looked exactly like the last dozen I'd tried.

Besides the low hum of the ship's engines, the droning snore of Nelvan's hologram was the only sound. I'd been flying so long, I couldn't really blame him for nodding off.

"You know, Captain," Blix yawned. "I've heard deep space freighters pass by this moon from time to time. You might get lucky and catch a ride one day."

A frustrated sigh was the only response I offered. My ship was nearly out of fuel, I was hopelessly lost in the dark caverns of a crazy, remote moon and my only chance to teleport out of here was almost gone.

The only bright spot was Jasette agreeing to stay with me. She'd missed her midday transport but arranged passage on the night shuttle. Even with the dark emptiness of the caverns, having her there with me, even as a hologram, was a great comfort.

A sputtering series of coughs and snorts signified Nelvan waking from his nap.

Nelvan yawned. "Hey, that looks different."

"What?" I couldn't tell where he was looking since his hologram was still blended with Blix and Jasette in the passenger seat.

"That tunnel above. We just passed it."

My hunch was that he dreamed the whole tunnel thing since he just woke up, but I was willing to take any chance at this point. I swung the ship around and brought the thrusters to the lowest setting.

Sure enough, there was a narrow tunnel in the ceiling, obscured by dense undergrowth. I backed the ship up and set the cannons on the undergrowth. The red beams opened up the passage in a few short freems, and a soft light shone down.

A thrill of hope went through me. I powered the ship forward and ascended into the tunnel. The steel walls of the circular passage gave me all the clues I needed that it headed out of these caverns.

"Nelvan, I'm promoting you." Just ahead was a well-lit curve in the steel tunnel.

"I didn't know I had a job title," Nelvan said.

"Of course. You were an ensign; now you're an officer."

"Officer Nelvan Flink," Nelvan said with awe. "I like the sound of that."

I maneuvered the ship around the bend and the bright, white glow of stars flooded into the cockpit.

"That has to be the surface of the moon." Jasette spoke with the same level of excitement that was pouring through me at the prospect of escape. The ship sped forward, the light at the end of the passage growing brighter as we ascended. We emerged in a high arc over the crater-pitted surface of a chalky white moon. The cockpit was alive with our victorious shouts.

With renewed energy, I piloted the craft across the surface of the moon, looking for any sign of the Iron Gauntlets.

A crackle of static came from my bracelet, followed by Forglyn's voice. "Most of you will see this on tomorrow's highlights but for those of you still watching, it looks like our captain has finally broken free of the moon caverns."

"That's right skrid," I said. "I made it."

"Let's not get ahead of ourselves," Forglyn said. "Only three jemmins left in the day."

"There." Jasette motioned to a flash of light in the distance. "See it?"

"Yeah." I headed toward the light. As we neared, I spied a glowing, white post planted in the moon's surface. The glimmer of metal necklaces hanging from the pole was the final confirmation that freedom was within reach. "That's it! Nothing can stop me now."

At that moment the ship buckled and swerved downward, and just before I crashed, I noticed it was completely out of fuel.

CHAPTER 20

Moon Walking
and Miscommunication

THE SPACESHIP SMASHED into the surface of the moon in a cloud of white dust.

"A most unfortunate turn of events for our captain." Forglyn announced over my bracelet. He seemed amused at my dire predicament. "And with only one jemmin left in the day, his chances don't look good."

The ship was lying sideways. I hit the cockpit hatch but the opening was stuck, so I sunk down in my seat and sent a few panic-driven kicks into the hatch. Around the fifth kick, there was a loud, crunching noise and the hatch lifted.

"Hurry, Glint," Jasette said.

I jumped to the dusty moon, my mind consumed with sprinting toward the glowing pole nearby—and that's when I noticed I couldn't breathe. Also, gravity was not my friend here. Every step was more of a slow, floating leap than the sprint I intended, and there was nothing in the air to keep me going. Under normal circumstances, I could've reached the pole in a few freems but with my new, bounding strides, progress was a torturous crawl. The sound of my speeding heartbeat flooded my ears.

"Ten freems left, ladies and gentlemen," Forglyn said.

My lungs burned for oxygen. I gave a final, two-legged thrust toward the pole. As I floated toward the necklace, my head started to spin. I reached out as far as my arm could stretch, praying I wasn't too late.

My hand grasped the Iron Gauntlet charm and putting aside the potential horrors of teleportation, I welcomed the jolt of energy as it lifted me away from this accursed moon.

Back at Glittronium, my return was far less dramatic. The visuals were off in the main room of Shansmannor Hall and the lights were dimmed. There were a few maintenance bots cleaning the wide expanse of the room in slow, synchronized sweeps. There wasn't even a hovering cambot to record my arrival. It was very anticlimactic, not to mention insulting, after escaping a horrific moon built by an insane doctor that I wanted to hurt badly.

I breathed deeply for several moments, thankful for the plentiful supply of oxygen. It offered me a chance to examine my new hands, with their thick layer of orange scales and retractable claws. A feeling of dread washed over me. The Enigma was turning me into a monster. There was no way to get rid of this necklace without someone else agreeing to wear it. And-even if I could somehow manage that, without the Enigma's protective power the chances of survival in the Iron Gauntlet were slim. I felt trapped on all sides. I was bound to the competition and bound to this cursed charm hanging from my neck like a noose. One thing was certain. If I survived this competition, I was getting rid of the Enigma the first chance I got.

The room seemed so vacant and lonely now that it was empty of the usual vibrant lights and throngs of excited fans. After so much time in those dark caverns, I didn't want any more dark, lonely places so I beat a quick path to the fore, but it did little to improve the situation. The lights were dim and much of the sparkling glitter was lost in the shadows. It seemed more like dead stones in the walls of a dark cave. Dozens of stoic guards flanked every passage to and from the room. They glanced in my direction as I neared but gave me little attention.

I kept a careful watch on the shadows for movement. Memories of Silvet's wraiths still haunted me. Any dark corner held the possibility that I was being watched. My only thought was to get back to my crew. A side door opened and I was greeted by their familiar faces, this time in person.

"Captain," Blix beamed. "You made it."

I shared some return embraces with my crew, forgetting momentarily about my 'no gushing displays of affection' guidelines for crew members. Although the hugs were made slightly awkward by my new lizard hands, I didn't care. I was just glad to be with real people again.

Nelvan stood at attention and saluted me. "Officer Nelvan reporting. Great to see you back, sir."

I shook my head. "Don't ever do that again." I gave him a grin and tousled his hair.

Jasette smiled at me for the first time in a long while. "Way to cut it close, Glint."

"Too close," I said.

"Just be glad you're not Dentrylich." Blix grimaced.

"The snake swordsman guy?" I said. "He didn't make it?"

"Activated the wrong lever." Blix gave a scolding look

my way. "Got swarmed by spine orbs. Eight skillful swords aren't enough against that kind of onslaught. I wouldn't recommend watching it on the replay." He shivered. "Grisly business."

I couldn't believe a powerful being like Dentrylich didn't escape that moon alive. I suddenly felt a lot more grateful to be standing in the darkened Shansmannor Hall foyer.

"You'd think with that finish I would've gotten a better reception," I said.

"Glittronium celebrities are quite regimented about their beauty sleep." Blix motioned to his face for reference. "I'm sure they'll edit you into the highlights tomorrow with a good deal of fanfare."

I cast a disappointed look around the room. "It's kind of depressing in here when the lights are off."

"Indeed," Blix said. "As the renowned poet Xottimer Cheelset spoke, 'Temporal shimmers, though grand to behold, are merely—'"

"No poetry," I broke in. "I'm tired and I have a headache."

Blix's eyes narrowed. "Fine. Come Officer Nelvan, you've an ear for artistry, don't you?"

"I love poetry," Nelvan said.

"Excellent." Blix smiled. "Goodnight Captain, get some rest for tomorrow's challenge." Blix led Nelvan toward the transverse cube as he started on a fresh batch of sentimental poetic garbage.

I turned to Jasette, feeling a little nervous now that it was just the two of us. There was still some weird tension hanging in the air and I wasn't sure how to break it.

"So ... you look nice."

Jasette held up her hands. "Please, Glint. No more awkward compliments."

"But you do."

A sad sort of smile came over her. "Listen, I have to leave tonight."

It felt like someone punched me in the heart. "But it's already late. Why not tomorrow? There's gotta be another transport and—"

She shook her head. "I think it's for the best."

After the cold loneliness of that crazy moon and the fear of almost being stuck there, the thought of her leaving was too much. I couldn't take it anymore.

I took her in my arms and looked deep into her eyes. "Please don't leave." I leaned in and kissed her. She tensed up at first, and then slowly relaxed into the kiss. She felt perfect next to me, like the missing piece of my life. It was by far the best moment since I arrived at Glittronium. All the worry and pain of the competition disappeared, and all that was left was this perfect moment.

Jasette drew back, brushing the electric blue hair from her face. Her deep green eyes were locked onto mine. "You sure aren't making this easy."

"Then don't go. I've already made it through two challenges. I'm doing great."

She raised an eyebrow.

"Okay, maybe not 'great' but I'm surviving. I think I could actually win this thing."

"I hope you do, Glint." She caressed the side of my face with her hand. "In the meantime, I have to think of the safety of my kingdom." She stepped back and took a deep breath.

"I want to help you with your search," I pleaded. "If it's important to you, it's important to me. Stay with me and when this is over, we'll go together."

"If that's true, why didn't you drop out of this competition and go with me instead of coming here."

There was a fresh ache in my heart. "I couldn't. I mean ... there's things I can't tell you right now. Just trust me that I had to do this."

She gave a sad nod. "Just like I have to take this transport tonight."

My brain struggled for words but came up empty. I just stood there feeling broken.

Jasette leaned in and kissed my cheek. "I'll be searching in the Krennis sector near Jelmontaire. Come find me when this is over."

My insides felt empty as I watched her head toward the transverse cube. She turned and gave a final wave as the doors closed behind her.

CHAPTER 21

JASETTE

Tales of a Space Princess

THE TRANSVERSE CUBE arrived at the 999th floor far too quickly. My head was still twisted from the conversation with Glint. I didn't want to see Forglyn or anyone else right now. But, he had my access pass for the transport, and I couldn't leave without it.

As strange as it was, I still wanted an excuse to delay departure from Glittronium. The duty to the people of my kingdom was a responsibility I didn't take lightly, but maybe I was rushing my decision. The thought of waiting another day or two and leaving with friends was a powerful reason for delay. After all, the help I would get from Glint and Blix and even sweet Nelvan might end up bringing me to the chrysolenthium flower faster than I could find it on my own.

The top floor of this monstrous building was a strange sight but not surprising given the self-important resident. The walls, ceilings, and floors of the hallways were spotless, seamless mirrors. The only embellishment that broke the pure, reflective surface was a series of diamond insets that flowed along the walls in perfect symmetry. Growing up in the royal family of Jelmontaire, I'd experienced my share of finery and glamour, but Glittronium sure knew how to push it to the extreme.

Even as a young girl, the thought of being primped and pampered in the royal dwelling of our crystal halo bored me to tears. I got the adventure bug early on. It was infinitely more thrilling to explore the sage forest beyond the kingdom or spar with the palace guard.

I paced the mirrored hallways, still processing my feelings for Glint. Sometimes it pained me to admit it, but despite his childish facade I knew deep down I had a strong connection with him. Those fleeting moments where he couldn't hide behind bravado, I'd seen a good man. Or at least, potential. Whether or not he could shed some of that clinging imma-turity and engage in a grown-up relationship was yet to be seen. But I wasn't ready to give up hope … yet.

Without realizing it, I found myself standing outside Forglyn's door. I pushed thoughts of Glint aside. I'd need more time to sort through those feelings later.

I took a quick look in the closest reflective surface—which wasn't difficult—to make sure I was put together. I ran my hands through my hair to give it some body and made a quick check of my teeth for any specks of food. It wasn't that I was interested in Forglyn, but it was always nice to show a jerk what he'd missed out on by being a player.

Right as I was about to hit the room panel, the door opened. Forglyn stood in the doorway, apparently well aware I had arrived.

He wore a snug, black V-neck that showcased his mus-cular frame.

"Jasette, so glad you came." His perfect teeth grinned at me. "Won't you come in?"

"Sure." I kept my reactions polite but curt. I didn't want to give him any ideas.

As I entered, it was hard not to be impressed with his suite. Everything was immaculate and stylish. The light ocean tones and casual décor immediately put me at ease. "Would you like some music?" He waved his hand and a traditional Jelmontaire folk song played softly in the background.

"Where did you get this?" I gave him a questioning look. "My grandmother used to play this song on her xyntholin."

He gave a bashful grin. "Well, after you left me gloons ago, I felt horrible. Like I'd taken you for granted. My therapist recommended I study up on your culture. She said it was a good way to develop more respect and esteem for someone I'd undervalued." I nodded but tried to keep my expression neutral. His words were speaking to me like the music in the background but his sincerity was still in question. "To my surprise, I fell in love with the native music of your culture. It moves me like little else."

"Music is very important on Jelmontaire," I said. "It has always been a part of my family."

Forglyn closed his eyes and breathed deeply. "I can see why. There's a richness in the tone and rhythm I don't often hear."

"I agree." I found myself sharing a warm smile with him and relaxing my composure. A warning signal flickered in my head. I straightened and cleared my throat. "So, you said you'd have the travel pass?"

"Yes, of course." He produced a small blue square from his pocket.

A part of me wanted to grab the pass and leave immediately. It meant returning to searching for the flower and the solitary life that I had grown so accustomed to. But now, the thought of going back to that life felt hollow. It meant leaving friendships that I'd begun to value. True, it was an odd group of friends I'd fallen in with but by some strange twist of cosmic forces, we'd been thrown together. The thought of leaving them now hit me in a painful rush. I couldn't quite explain it, but I knew at that moment I wanted to stay.

"Forglyn," I said. "I know I already delayed this morning's transport, but I'm not sure I'm ready to leave."

A crinkle line of concern formed between his eyes. "Is everything alright?"

"Yes. I just don't think I'm ready yet."

"Are you sure? Tonight's transport is our finest. Luxury travel at its best. If you wait, I can't promise what you'll get."

"It's okay. I've flown in plenty of clunkers over the gloons."

"You're absolutely sure?" His eyes went serious and lines of concern formed on his brow. "You seemed quite ready to go yesterday. It's usually a good idea to go with your first impulse."

"I'm sure."

He gave a thoughtful nod. "Very well." He moved to a narrow table nearby. "Perhaps we can make a toast to your decision."

He made a gesture to a table next to us. Two slender glasses emerged, along with a platter of delicacies presented with the style and artistry of a master chef.

"Essence of gliss fruit imported from Jelmontaire," he said. "And some of the finer delicacies Glittronium has to offer."

It was my favorite drink and I couldn't remember if I'd ever mentioned it to him in the past. The aroma of finely prepared food wafted over, enticing me to try a few.

"Thank you, Forglyn but I'm not really hungry." I was starving. I'd missed my evening meal because I was busy trying to help Glint navigate out of those caves. But hunger would have to wait. I had to keep things professional and make my visit short.

"I understand." Forglyn cast a disappointed look at the floor. "I suppose my actions in the past leave little room for trust." He grabbed a glass of gliss fruit and took a small sip. "You know, I haven't had this since I last saw you. I forgot how ..." He fixed me with a warm look, "exquisite everything was."

There was a chance I was being too hard on him. After all, gliss fruit was my planet's claim to fame. One of the most popular exports we were known for. "You should try my father's special vintage."

"I should be so lucky." He smiled and took another drink. "Well, I suppose I should arrange for a later transport. I'll have to pull a few strings but it shouldn't be too much trouble." He put down his glass and cast a sad look at the table. "I apologize for keeping you."

"Wait, Forglyn." I grabbed the other glass. "I admit I can't put the past aside but I appreciate your efforts." I lifted the glass to him. "Here's to new beginnings."

He smiled broadly and lifted his glass. "To new beginnings."

We both took a drink. The rich, earthy flavor reminded me of home. I'd been away far too long.

"I hope you don't mind," he said. "When I thought you were leaving tonight, I got you a going-away present."

"Oh, no, that's okay," I shook my head.

"No, please." Forglyn's eyes pleaded with me. "I put a lot of effort into this. Think of it as my final bid for your forgiveness."

"It's really not necessary."

"It's a gift for your family." He spoke with sincerity. "For your kingdom."

Something was definitely different about him. I couldn't put my finger on it. He was either reformed or insane. I wasn't ready to trust him but if he had something that could help my family, it was at least worth a look.

"What is it?" I said.

He headed for a glossy white door. "Something you've been looking for." Forglyn hit a panel and the door slid away. A darkened room lay beyond.

I headed closer to see what was in the room.

Forglyn hit another control and a light shone down on a shimmering object hovering on a waist high pedestal. It looked like a flower. A sudden hope sprang up within me.

I stared at it for a moment, speechless. I turned to him, "Is that ... that can't be what I think it is."

His expression was sincere. "I heard of your kingdom's need," he said. "I wanted to help."

I stared at the flower in amazement. "A chrysolenthium flower. How did you find it?"

He gave a playful shrug. "I have my ways."

Mesmerized by the object of my long quest, I walked into the darkened room. The crystalline petals shimmered in the spotlight. My eyes grew dizzy looking at the myriad of sparkles that danced across its surface. I felt myself sway and took a wide step to keep my balance.

"Everything alright, Jasette?" Forglyin stood in the darkened doorway, watching me.

My head started to spin. I took another awkward step and dropped my glass. The sharp sound of it shattering on the floor suddenly brought clarity to my situation.

"Perhaps you should sit down." Forglyn spoke in a detached sort of way.

My fingers fumbled over my power suit controls. I activated the stimulant enhancers and felt my body stabilize. I turned and stood tall. I drew my silver laser pistols and pointed them at his soon-to-be wounded torso.

"You are resourceful, aren't you?" He said.

"You devious creep." I let loose a barrage of red beams. High-tech holo-shield tiles emerged around him, diffusing my blasts.

"Temper, temper." He wagged his finger at me.

Holding clasps burst from the ceiling. The cold metal wrapped tightly around my wrists and ankles. My pistols clattered to the ground. Forglyn strode toward me, motioning to the sparkling flower. "I'm afraid this flower isn't real." He moved his hand through the realistic looking hologram. "But my eventual takeover of your planet is."

He stopped in front of me and gave a wicked smile. I wanted to round kick the perfect teeth right out of his head.

"Being a celebrity has granted many luxuries," he said. "But it's time to expand my power and your planet is ripe for the picking. Consider it payback for daring to leave me gloons ago."

"So that's why Glint is a contestant? To lure me here and exact some demented sense of revenge?"

Forglyn laughed. "No, unfortunately the supercomputer picked that surly fool. But his continual survival has caused me considerable grief." A look of rage crossed his face, like only Glint can inspire. "My powerful associates make a great deal of money from this competition. The bets placed on guaranteed winners must be assured or my clients become very displeased. I can't have you or anyone else helping him survive another challenge. I was going to let you leave tonight on that transport. But you refused my generous offer and stayed to help that buffoon. You brought this on yourself."

I struggled against the holding clasps but I was held fast.

Forglyn leaned closer. "I've been planning to expand my power for some time now. The winnings I make from this competition will give me the resources I need to expand my presence in the galaxy. Even your friends might make for a good profit on the black market. That boy Nelvan seems to have no records. I'm sure he'll fetch a high price."

"Leave him alone!" I threatened.

He sneered. "You can't stop me. My power and influence have been building for some time now. Soon even Mar Mar the Unthinkable will be awed by my strength in the galaxy. Your arrival here merely inspired Jelmontaire as my choice of planets to overtake. You should feel honored."

I spat in his face. "I can't wait to see Glint win this wretched show and watch your pathetic little plans crumble to nothing."

He wiped the spit from his cheek, his face turning dark. "I assure you, that will never happen." He waved his hand and the metal clasps lifted me into darkness.

CHAPTER 22

NELVAN

Tales of
a Time-Traveling Teen

"SHALL I BEGIN THE WAKE CYCLE, SIR?" Chendrick said.

"Yeah, I'm up." I jumped off the hover sleeper and stretched deeply. I'd never really had a problem getting a good night's sleep, but these future beds made it even better. The warm gel was like a soft massage as you slept. It made my cot at the science academy seem like sleeping on a rock.

My silver academy jumpsuit lay folded on the chair nearby. Once again, it had been cleaned while I slept. I stepped into the only clothes that reminded me of the Earth I knew and zipped it tight.

I took out the small, metal replica of an airplane I kept in the back pouch. It was the only thing I had from my mom. She gave it to me right before I left for science academy. I turned it over in my hand, missing home and the distant past I used to be a part of.

I quickly stuffed it back in my pouch, not wanting to dwell on sad things. This future—crazy as it is—was my life now, and I had better get used to it. Like my mom always said, "The future is wide open—better to embrace it and make the best of things than spend your life worrying in the shadows." Of course, she was always one to jump into new things with both feet. I was a bit more reserved, so it was hard to live life by her mottos.

I threw on my new brown jacket and zipped it half way. I took a look in the room mirror. It was a good look for me. My new look for a new future.

Chendrick, my room computer, was letting in sunlight and changing the soft night music to something more energetic.

"Hey, Chendrick," I said. "What was that song you played yesterday? Y'know, the one I liked."

"The music style was sky tremors, sir," Chendrick said. "You said it reminded you of cultural music known as rock and roll."

"Yeah, play that. And can you make more of those sweet breads and crispy meats for breakfast?"

"Certainly, sir. I'll have it ready in the front room."

"Thanks, Chendrick." Homesick as I was, I had to admit this place was awesome. Not only was this the biggest, nicest room I'd ever stayed in, but you could order any kind of food whenever you wanted. It was like a dream.

A soft tone sounded. "Sir, your associate Blix has arrived."

"Great, let him in." I jogged into the front room to find Blix walking through the doorway. I was still getting used to the fact that a hulking, lizard man was my friend.

"Good morning, Nelvan. Sleep well?"

"It's hard not to. These beds are incredible."

Blix gave a sour look upward. "What is this horrid music?"

"Sky tremors." I moved my head to the fast rhythm. "Isn't it great?"

He shook his head. "To each his own."

"You want some breakfast?" I made a beeline to the circular dining table. It was already filled with a great-smelling meal.

"Thank you, no."

After a quick prayer, I started in on the delicious food.

"Decided to stick with the jacket, did we?" Blix said.

I nodded between bites.

Blix sighed and casually made his way to the table. "Did you hear about the break-in?"

I shook my head and took a bite of a jelly-filled bread.

"Another attempt at the Iron Gauntlet vault." Blix rubbed his chin. "This would-be thief is quite determined. I heard nine levels of security were compromised before the alarm chased him off again."

"He sounds dangerous." A line of jelly rolled down my chin. I rubbed it off with the back of my hand. "I wouldn't want to meet him."

"Indeed. Thieves are not to be trusted."

I nodded and took another bite.

"Have you heard from Jasette?" Blix said.

"No, not today."

"Hmm." Blix seemed preoccupied. "Very odd."

"What?"

He shrugged. "Probably nothing." He took the Bible out of his satchel and laid it on the table. "Bible study this morning?"

"Yeah, sure." I piled some of the thin, crispy meat strips

on my plate. "Don't you think we should tell the captain about these studies? He's kind of weird about it."

Blix chuckled. "Whatever for? Do you like seeing him rant and rave?"

"No but, I dunno. I feel weird hiding it from him."

"Nonsense." Blix started flipping through the pages. "It's not a secret, we just haven't mentioned it. Trust me, he has enough on his mind with the competition."

"I guess so." I chewed on a meat strip. "But when the contest is over, we should tell him."

Blix leaned back and smiled. "I must say, your candor is most refreshing and a testament to this book. It reminds me how jaded 853 gloons have made me."

I looked down, feeling embarrassed. I always felt his compliments were more than I deserved. I knew I had plenty of maturing to do before I lived up to my faith. "I dunno, I've got lots to work on."

Blix gave me a dismissive wave.

We spent breakfast reading about how the apostles were imprisoned for their faith. Blix retold his experience of spending two gloons in the salt mines as a slave to the dragon lords of the Krelvorcian sector. He had a tendency to repeat stories, but I didn't mind. Each time he told them he would add something new or tell it in such a way that it related to what we were going through. I was definitely glad to have a friend like him in this strange, new future.

We met the captain in the foyer. He looked like he'd had a rough night's sleep.

"You okay, Captain?" I said.

He gave a slow nod. There was a detached and weary look in his eyes. Sometimes I felt like he put too much on his shoulders. "Either of you hear from Jasette this morning?"

Blix shook his head. "I guess she took the transport after all. My decision matrix must need altering. I predicted at least another day's delay."

The captain straightened, his expression looking numb. "Well, that's that. Come on, we've got a competition to win."

I gave him an encouraging pat on the back. "Good luck today, Captain. You can do this. I'll be praying for you."

A weary kind of smile animated his face, and he put a hand on my shoulder. "Thanks, kid."

We headed into the darkened main room. Inside there were throngs of people and every kind of alien imaginable. The amazing visuals that brought the room to life showed dark parts of space with few stars. There were several swirling space formations. They were dark and eerie looking, but there was something awe-inspiring about them.

"Vortex clusters." Blix nodded as he scanned the room. "An ominous tone to set for the day's challenge."

"Stop trying to scare me." The captain said.

"Greetings." Forglyn strolled up beside us wearing a dark suit peppered with subtle, white sparkles. "Hope you slept well, Glint. Today's challenge is not for the faint of heart."

I saw the vein in the captain's neck throbbing. "You heard anything from Jasette?" The captain gave Forglyn a dark look.

"Oh." Forglyn smirked. "She didn't tell you?"

"Tell me what?"

"Well, I begged her to stay, but she insisted on leaving last night. Something about a missing flower."

The captain's expression was blank. He was quiet for a few moments.

"So she did leave." He managed.

"I'm afraid so," Forglyn said. "These things happen. I'm sure it will all work out."

A bright pedestal shone underneath him, and he lifted high above us.

"Welcome one and all," his voice boomed throughout the room. "To the third challenge of the Iron Gauntlet."

The crowd cheered and the death march sent tremors through the floor.

"Today's surprise twist is very unique," he said. "As you know, time travel has been outlawed for nearly a century. But since the universal security time lords are big fans of the show …" Forglyn motioned to a wide platform raised in the air. A white cloth was lifted off three oval-shaped objects that resembled doorways. A glowing white energy swirled inside. "We've been granted a limited and temporary window into the past of our remaining contestants."

A ripple of oohs and ahhs filled the room.

"They will be transported to a dark time from their cultural history." Forglyn motioned to a large vortex behind him. It began to swirl faster and grow in size. "Once they arrive, the ancestors they find themselves surrounded by hold the key to return. The challenge for our contestants is to find the one ancestor we've secretly chosen and say the mystery phrase that will cause the Iron Gauntlet to appear and pull them back through the time portal."

The captain narrowed his eyes. "What does that even mean?"

Blix had a studied expression as though lost in thought. "Indeed. Quite a puzzler."

A pedestal lit up under the captain and began to raise him up.

He frowned at Blix. "Thanks for the help."

"There's one source of help for our contestants," Forglyn continued. "Every jemmin, they will be allowed visual contact with their entourage. However, due to the relative properties of time, one jemmin for us will be one montul for them. If they let too much time go by, they may find themselves trapped with their ancestors in a turbulent past."

Excited whispers spread through the crowd. The captain, Chak, and Chessandrillia were now positioned in front of their respective time portals.

"And now, contestants." Forglyn motioned to the portals. "Prepare to meet your ancestors and speak the mystery phrase to the chosen one—or remain there forever!"

The energy in the time portals swirled faster, and the contestants were forcefully drawn into them. The crowd erupted in cheers.

"What happens now?" I looked up at Blix.

"A dark time in your Earth's past?" Blix shook his head. "Let's pray the captain maintains his sanity."

Selinxia walked up to us. "Glint's connection room is right this way."

She led us to a side door in the main room. The décor was dark purple and black with plush-looking furniture. Miniature point lights were set in artistic patterns, making it look like a group of fireflies had been frozen in flight.

There was a large viewing screen at one end with comfy

chairs placed before it. A table filled with exotic-looking refreshments was the centerpiece of the room.

"He should be on screen in about forty freems," she said. "Keep in mind, for him an entire montul has passed."

"Understood." Blix appeared as if this was all normal for him.

"Please let me know if you need anything." Selinxia smiled and left the room.

"Get ready, Nelvan." Blix tapped me on the shoulder.

The screen flickered to life. The captain was sitting on a simple cot in a small room where everything looked very grey and plain. He wore a stiff, dark suit and tie. For once he looked clean-shaven and well groomed. His expression, however, seemed worried and desperate.

"Blix? Nelvan?" His eyes darted between us. "Is that really you?"

"Yes, Captain." Blix spoke hurriedly. "What can you tell us of your situation?"

"It's horrible." His eyes went wide. "I'm in some kind of old Earth prison called the FremmelTech Corporation. They make me slave away in a tiny, grey-walled cell called a cubicle. I have to repeat the same tasks every day, mindlessly entering nearly identical information into ancient electronics."

Blix gasped. "That sounds awful."

"Not to mention this horrible uniform that chokes me all day." He held up a thin tie as if it was a noose. "Plus, look at these." He held up glove-covered hands. "I have to keep my freak, lizard hands covered and my wings tucked under my coat so they don't think I'm some kind of mutant. I had to pretend it was all part of a costume when I first got here."

"I'm sorry, Captain," Blix said. "Bad fashion is its own punishment."

"I'm stuck here all day," the captain pleaded. "They keep our food and sleeping chambers in the same building. They call it an employee perk that we never have to leave and my fellow prisoners actually believe it!"

Blix shook his head. "Poor deluded souls."

"What year is it on Earth, Captain?" I said.

"2050," the captain said. "And if I don't escape this horrid past soon, I'm gonna lose it."

"Focus, Captain," Blix said. "You need to find the mystery person and speak the mystery phrase if you ever hope to return."

The captain threw up his hands. "I still have no idea what that means."

The screen started to flicker.

"Gather as much information as you can," Blix said. "There must be a clue somewhere. See you in another montul."

The captain gave an angry look at Blix as the visual went black.

Blix turned to me and smiled. "That went well."

I frowned. "It did?" I thought it went terribly. It seemed to me like the captain was in the exact same spot as before.

Blix shrugged. "Well, he's alive. That's always a good sign."

"I suppose. I just wish I knew how to help."

"Indeed. Let's think about this." Blix grabbed a pastry from the snack table and popped it in his mouth.

I racked my brain, thinking of what we could do. The captain had landed on earth twenty years, or gloons as they call them now, before the time I came from. Sadly, I had spent little time on history studies. I'd been obsessed with technology and where the future would take us. I guess it was ironic I ended up a century after my time.

A possible solution came to me. "Maybe he could try common phrases. Y'know, try them out on the people around him."

Blix nodded. "Process of elimination. Yes, that's plausible. Although, the sheer number of possibilities and the pool of potential recipients would take longer than his time allows. Plus, those around him would no doubt find that behavior strange and stop talking to him altogether. That would eliminate any chance of return."

I nodded. I had to think of something else.

"Wait." Blix snapped his fingers. "I have it."

"Really? What?"

"Well, it requires a bit of technology, but even primitive forms should suffice."

The screen flickered on again. The captain didn't look well. His drab, dark suit was loose and wrinkled, and his hair was disheveled. There were dark circles under his eyes and he looked as though he'd gained some weight.

"So glad you're alive," Blix said cheerily. "Have you figured anything out?"

The captain stared at us with tired eyes. "So grey ... cold ... lonely."

"Captain, pay attention," Blix said. "I know how you can get back."

That seemed to stir him from his daze a bit. "Really?"

"Yes, I know how you can find the mystery person."

The captain stared at Blix, the old fierceness in his eyes. "Tell me now!"

"First, you'll need to gather some electronics. Nothing fancy, just a few rudimentary computer units."

The captain nodded in an excited manner. "I can do that. What else?"

"Next, a simple rewiring and programming should allow you to construct a time displacement sensor. The mystery person is obviously linked to the time rift you're currently inhabiting. The time signature should be unmistakable and the sensor will lead you right to him."

Blix leaned back, hands behind his head, and smiled broadly.

The captain stared at him, his expression blank. "Um, construct a what now?"

Blix frowned. "Time displacement sensor."

"How would I know how to do that?"

"It's common knowledge."

The screen started to flicker.

"Good luck, Captain." Blix waved.

The captain looked as though he were about to launch into an angry tirade when the visual went to black.

Blix rubbed his chin. "Too bad. That probably would have worked."

"It sounded good to me," I said. "Too bad he didn't land in my time. I could've helped him alter the time travel units to make them functional."

"Yes, although your coordinates were quite faulty. You ended up countless gloons and several galaxies away from where you intended."

He was painfully correct. "True."

Blix grabbed another pastry from the table. "Perhaps we should concentrate on a non-technical method."

I nodded. We sat for several moments in thought. The pressure of coming up with a solution in such a short amount of time was making it difficult to think. After a long moment of silence I turned to Blix, hoping he was having better luck.

"Any ideas?" I said.

Blix gave a sad shake of his head. "Let's hope the captain figured something out."

The screen flickered on. The captain sat slumped in a grey chair in his darkened room. He was looking down with a vacant stare.

"Captain? Hello?" Blix waved at the screen.

The captain slowly looked up at us. He appeared to be in a trance. "Blix? Nelvan?"

"Hi, Captain." I answered with enthusiasm, hoping to break him out of his spell.

He simply stared at me and yawned.

"Captain," Blix said. "There's not much time. Have you learned anything?"

"Yes." The captain spoke as though he was drugged. "If I work very hard for the next five years, I could become the junior associate to the assistant supervisor. Isn't that great?" His expression was blank.

Blix gave me a worried glance. "Start praying," he whispered. "Quick."

I sent up an emergency prayer for the captain. He sure looked like he could use it. I'd never seen him so drained. Usually he was just plain difficult. *Difficult.* That gave me an idea.

"Captain," I said. "Is there anyone there that seems really

difficult? All these challenges are made to be difficult. Maybe they made the mystery person the hardest one to deal with."

A look of anger crossed the captain's face. "You know who's difficult? My boss."

"Yes, let's explore Nelvan's idea." Blix leaned toward the screen. "I recommend a series of carefully planned run-ins with your boss that seem like happenstance. Engage in conversation immediately. Deliver several phrases that seem like ordinary banter and chart your progress. Then, you must—"

"Yeah." The captain stood. The old fire returning to his eyes. "I should talk to that filthy skrid right now." He flung off his tie and started pulling off his drab suit.

"No, that's not what I meant," Blix waved his hands as if wiping away the thought. "Okay, let's go through this step by step."

Glint pulled open a drawer and retrieved his old clothes. Blix continued with his step-by-step breakdown of conversational strategy, but the captain didn't seem to be listening anymore. Soon he was back in the outfit I'd grown so used to seeing him wear.

"Did you get all that?" Blix said. "We should probably do a quick review."

The captain clenched his jaw and made fists. "I got it. I'll go tell that scumbag what I should have told him the first day."

"No, wait!" Blix leaned forward, reaching toward the captain like he could stop him.

Glint stormed away from the screen, muttering to himself.

Blix slumped back on the couch. He gave a sad look my way. "This is not good."

Suddenly the screen switched to a view of the main room.

The captain was standing right next to Forglyn and the crowd was cheering.

"Look who's the first to arrive," Forglyn announced. "Captain Starcrost."

I shared a surprised look with Blix.

Forglyn patted the captain on the back. "The captain's mystery person was his boss and the mystery phrase was 'I quit.' How did you figure it out?"

The captain gave a hesitant grin. "Um ... just lucky, I guess."

Blix and I rushed back into the main room to welcome the captain home. He was still pretty out of it, but he seemed very relieved to be back.

We helped him up to his room, and Blix suggested we leave so he could get some rest. Although it was still the same morning as when he left, for the captain a few months, or montuls as they call them, had passed. No doubt he needed some recovery time.

We left the room and Blix said we probably shouldn't mention anything about our study of the imprisoned apostles, as it may have had something to do with that challenge the captain recently endured. His strange Vythian abilities still confused me, so I figured it was best for now to agree.

Blix headed for his room, telling me it was high time to unravel a building anomaly. I had no idea what he was talking about but he seemed really preoccupied, so I told him I'd meet him later.

When I got back to my room, it was dark. Usually the lights flicked on the moment I stepped through the door.

"Chendrick," I said, "can you turn on the lights?"

There was no answer. The room was quiet. I had a strange

sensation that I wasn't alone. Suddenly there was a sharp prickle on the side of my neck that felt like a bee sting. A wave of dizziness swept over me.

I turned to run from my room, but my legs felt like they were stuck in thick mud. I was about to pass out and there was nothing I could do to stop it. I said a quick prayer for protection as I crumpled to the floor.

CHAPTER 23

BLIX

*Tales of
a Refined Vythian*

EVENTS ALWAYS FORM A PATTERN no matter how random they may seem at the outset. There is a certain momentum and rhythm to the universe.

The conceptual musings of such illusory patterns generally resolve in poetic verse or thoughtful song, merely acknowledging the existence of an interwoven reality. A far more practical application is employed by astute professionals, who analyze the results to predict everything from financial investments to apprehending criminal masterminds.

The pattern is fluid by nature and difficult to chart, as constant alterations must be made. I am, admittedly, a novice in the predictive art. At the moment, I wished my skills were more advanced, as the pattern of my current circumstances was heading toward a decidedly negative resolution.

I wandered through the pomp and circumstance of the competition after party looking slightly aloof due to my preoccupied mental musings. This, of course, had the beneficial result of helping me fit right in with the exclusive party attendees.

I was hoping the excitement of social interaction and lavish Glittronium fanfare would loosen the mental knots. I was missing some crucial bit of information. That final key to unlocking the full discovery of the pattern of events.

The main illumination for the after party came from a giant, luminous, sim jellyfish undulating from the domed ceiling. It cast a spectrum of purple lights on the glamorous guests. The long tentacles of the jellyfish swayed in slow, whip-like motions through the crowd, temporarily highlighting guests in vivid purple.

The simulated scene brought back a memory of the day I almost died.

I was marooned on the seventh moon of the planet Screnthin. I was sent there by the squid czar of Screnthin after besting him in quad-level, quantum chess. I'd thought it was a friendly game, but after my victory it turned out the squid leader was far more sensitive and vindictive than I'd hoped. He wasted little time banishing me to the seventh moon with no supplies.

The purple moon was desolate and hot. The terrain was rocky and strewn with thorn-filled vines. Sustenance was difficult to come by. I was at the tail end of a trying montul of survival on the moon. I was severely weakened by the lack of food and my spirit was broken. That's when a multi-limbed Krivett attacked me. The vicious, armor-plated bug encircled me with its serpentine body and poison-spewing tendrils. In my weakened condition, I held little doubt this was my final moment.

That's when energy blasts tore into the Krivett's antennae, its only weakness, and it went crawling back to a dark hole. Low and behold, when I sought out my deliverer, there was

Captain Starcrost. He stood there in the thorny jungle, clad in his atmosphere suit, the barrel of his DEMOTER still smoking.

It was an impulsive act of bravery on his part, but it hinted at a noble spirit inside. There have been many times since when I have doubted that assumption, but when I glimpse it now and again I am reassured.

It took some convincing that I meant him no harm, and after a promise of three hundred vibes for a ride to the nearest spaceport, we were in his star freighter headed off the deadly purple moon.

He eventually convinced me to stay aboard for a while. Though his intentions of securing a strong ally were purely of a selfish nature, the randomness of exploring the galaxies with a rootless space drifter held an adventurous appeal.

The unlikeliest of kinships was forged over the gloons and I must admit, despite the frustration his impulsive nature can bring, it is a life that suits me well.

I drifted back to the present, my eyes wandering across the room. A few hover screens displaying competition high-lights circled overhead like lazy vultures. An ice carving of a huge space serpent wound through the room, showcasing an endless array of epicurean delights.

Never one to shy away from gourmet fare, I zeroed in on a spiraling tower of crab cakes. I popped a few in my mouth and chewed slowly. Closing my eyes, I delighted in the savory cuisine. One of the main drawbacks to adventuring through the stars with a broke space drifter is the lack of fine foods.

There was a multi-layered silver tray of caramel treats just ahead. The excitement got the better of me and I ended up bumping into a short old man with a thin spiral of white hair I hadn't noticed in my quest for sweets.

He arched back as he took in my full stature and gasped. "Oh my, Chakdragonnon." His pale blue eyes were filled with fear. His hands fumbled about his maroon, pinstriped suit as if looking for a weapon, then folded in a supplicating gesture as if thinking better of that course of action. "P-Please don't hurt me. I'm one of your fans. A big supporter of your assured victory."

I waved my hand and assumed a dignified stance. "You're mistaken. My name is Blix. Vythian kind certainly, but far more cultured than my brethren Chak."

The old man put a hand to his heart and seemed to deflate with relief. "Oh, marvelous. Yes, of course. I've seen you with that Starcrost fellow. Part of his entourage, aren't you?"

I nodded, wondering how long this polite conversation would have to continue before I indulged in the caramel treats mere steps away. "Indeed. Well, nice to meet you, I'm sure you're very busy so—"

"Oh, I do apologize for cheering on another competitor." He grabbed my arm to communicate sincerity, then shivered and drew back his hand as if he wasn't sure I was safe. "You won't take it personally now, will you?"

"Not at all." I smiled broadly, careful not to show any sharp teeth to frighten him further. "It's all part of the competition."

"Yes, yes, good." His nervous eyes darted across the throwing knives criss-crossed on my torso. "You're sure now? No hard feelings? It's just that my associates and I have placed a rather large wager on Chak. I meant no disrespect."

"My good man, that's perfectly ... What did you say?"

Something triggered in my mind, another wrinkle in the emerging pattern.

The old man stiffened, the worried look returning. "Oh dear. What did I say? I didn't mean it, whatever it was."

I couldn't speak for a moment, my mental faculties commanding full attention. The cyborg ambush in the captain's room was the first obvious thread of incongruence. I'd thought little of it at the time, as allowances must be made for the random chaotics of intersecting lines. However, after the abrupt and uncharacteristic departure of Jasette, I was confident a stark new pattern was already in full effect. This latest revelation only fueled the resolution of the paradigm.

The old man was backing away slowly, hands held defensively before him. "I changed my mind. I'm cheering for your Starcrost associate. Yes, indeed. Victory for Starcrost." He pumped his fist in the air in a feeble cheer.

"That's not necessary," I held out a reassuring hand.

At the sight of my reaching hand he let out a yelp, then turned and ran into the crowd.

I grabbed a handful of caramels and headed out of the room. My mind was sending out warning signals that things were moving fast, and my reactions were far too sluggish.

The transverse cube whisked me up to the 444th floor, and I grabbed the communicator on the way to my room. I checked the time readout. The day was coming to a close.

I activated my communicator and sent a distress call to Nelvan. The light band swirled around the device for several moments as if visually scolding my late actions. I chided myself for being so blind to an obvious chain of events. My pattern-predicting contemporaries would be ashamed.

Suddenly, my communicator lit up. A cursory check of the tone variant identified the captain as the source.

"Captain." I answered with a sense of urgency that I hoped would communicate our dire situation. "No time to lose. The lines are intersecting toward a negative outcome. We're in trouble."

"Thanks for the news flash, genius," he said.

He was in a belligerent mood, even more than usual. Obviously, he was suffering the subconscious effects of being caught in the negative flow of a resolving pattern.

I reached my room and waved my bracelet in front of the control panel. The door dissolved and I hurried inside.

"Hello, sir." Sorkell, my room computer, greeted me. "Shall I prepare your evening scale smoothing treatment?"

"No time, Sorkell," I said.

"What was that?" The captain's voice sounded from the communicator.

"Nothing, my room computer." I headed for my sleeping chamber to gather supplies. "Listen Captain, you don't understand the danger we face."

"I'm the one stuck in these life-and-death challenges. I understand perfectly."

I was feeling desperate, knowing my time was running out. "Listen, it's very important that you listen to every word I'm about to tell you."

A harsh beep sounded on my communicator, followed by broken bits of static. Fragments of the captain's voice were intermingled with the static.

"Captain?" I spoke close to the communicator. "Can you hear me?"

A long stream of static was my only answer. I tried to send an emergency thought message, but the pressure on my temples told me it was being blocked.

"Blix," Sorkell said. "You have a visitor."

My time was up. I was thoroughly disappointed in my performance. There was no salvaging the situation now.

I straightened my dagger straps, held my head high and made my way to the door of my room, resigned to my fate. Escape from Glittronium security, at least in my current location, was highly improbable.

I activated the door panel and was immediately hit with a bright holding ray. The technological power was intense. I would've been more curious as to the advanced construction behind the power if I wasn't in so much pain.

My body arched in natural response to the surge of energy. Having experienced a fair amount of pain over the centuries, I'd developed methods of mental detachment that made it more tolerable. But pain is still pain, and I prayed for the moment to be over soon.

Through a great deal of effort, I looked down at my captor. As I suspected, Forglyn stood before me, security bots hovering over him, assaulting me with their holding rays. There was a squad of helmeted guards filling the hallway behind him.

It was exceedingly difficult to speak but I couldn't resist a final attempt to erode his confidence. "You can't win. I've examined all strands of pattern resolution. They all end badly for you." It was pure deception of course, but I hoped it was enough to throw him off his game.

His face tightened with anger. Forglyn motioned to the

guards, who quickly swarmed around me. They applied several holding clasps about my body that were armed, no doubt, with powerful nerve toxins. The clasps activated and I felt my body thankfully slip away from the pain and into unconsciousness.

CHAPTER 24

GLINT

Tales of a Space Captain

THE ANNOUNCEMENT that the final challenge of the Iron Gauntlet was to take place at sundown sent an excited buzz through Shansmannor Hall. Everyone seemed to be thrilled with the surprise twist that the challenge was rescheduled and would start in less than a trid. Everyone, that is, except the competitor that was about to die, AKA me.

As I walked the halls, the visuals spread generously throughout the building showcased the latest competition recap. Along with the news that the challenge time had been moved up, the latest competition casualty was reported—apparently Chessandrillia never made it back from the latest challenge. She was taken to a time in her planet's past where the mind hive met resistance from the larva vortex, and a great rift was formed that resulted in a cosmic morph reverberation. The Iron Gauntlet special-effects team recreated the highlights of the grisly event in stomach-churning detail. With only two competitors left and the final challenge looming ever closer, I was in full panic mode.

To make matters worse, my crew was missing.

I'd spent the last trid searching for them with zero luck. The security guards in this place were worthless. When I got back to my room, it never felt so empty.

"Any word, Jenson?" I said.

"I'm sorry, sir. No contact from your friends or security. Although they do tell me they are looking into the situation very thoroughly."

"Yeah, right. You believe that line of trash?"

"Sir, for one of the top two competitors in the Iron Gauntlet, I believe the request for increased vigilance is quite reasonable."

I looked at the ceiling and nodded in agreement with my awesome room computer. "You should be running things in this place, Jenson."

"You give me too much credit, sir."

I went to the room interface and hit the control panel for the building concierge. A teen boy with a spotless, crisp uniform emerged on the screen. He stood at attention, his hands folded neatly on the desk before him. He was wearing pulsating eye enhancers, an annoying trend I'd noticed among the Glittronium youth.

He broke into a toothy grin. "How may I be of service, Mr. Starcrost?"

"*Captain* Starcrost. You can start by wiping that phony smile off your face and getting me the head of security."

"Terribly sorry, *Captain*." His face slid back into his toothy smile again. I could tell that this time it was just to spite me. "I've been asked to tell you our security forces are already doing their utmost to look into your situation."

"Really? Then where's my crew?"

"I understand your concerns," his eyes flashed and he gave an insincere nod. "We apologize for the inconvenience. Your issue is very important to us. Please be patient while—"

I slammed my fist into the control panel, ending the visual connection, but I was denied the satisfying crunch of broken electronics. The clear, protective coating merely absorbed the force, bending like rubber around my knuckles, then snapped back in place like I'd never touched it.

I spun around, eyeing an ivory sculpture of a three-headed warrior with dual blades, raised and ready to strike. I drew the DEMOTER X and sent a beautiful blast of energy into its torso. The sculpture exploded into a shower of white fragments and floating dust.

"Excellent shot, sir," Jenson said. "I can have another sculpture readied for disposal at your request."

I holstered the weapon. "You're the only one who really gets me, Jenson."

I stormed from the room, wondering whether a crew of robot Jensons wouldn't be such a bad idea.

After another sickening ride down the transverse cube, I was at the main floor, heading for the security office. As I passed the concierge desk, the teen boy recognized me. He walked toward me, holding up his hands as if to stop my progress.

"Sir, you can't go back there," the boy said. "Look, I've already told you that—"

I drew the DEMOTER and leveled it at his head without breaking stride. "Back off, freak eyes."

He froze, holding up his hands.

I kicked open the door of the security room and marched up to the desk. Grilg, the goateed guard that had shown up at my room the night of the cyborg attack, was manning the counter. His expression went from boredom to panic. His fingers fumbled over the controls of his forearm computer as I drew near. I grabbed him by his black jacket and yanked him toward me.

"Where's my crew?" I barked at him.

Just moments ago I'd eaten a sandwich loaded with onions. I hoped the pungent smell was hitting him full force. His repulsed grimace gave me assurance of my goal.

"Sir," he coughed. "We're doing everything we can to—"

"Well, do more." I gripped his jacket tighter. My new thick lizard hands were crumpling his jacket nicely.

"Alright." He patted my hands either as a reassurance or a signal that my grip was too tight. "I'll put another guard detail on it."

"Three more!"

"Okay, just stop twisting my coat. It stings."

There was a soft tone and a screen behind Grilg lit up. Forglyn appeared on the visual. His attention was fixated on adjusting his metallic silver tie.

He gave a casual glance our way. "Is there a problem down there?"

"Yeah." I dropped Grilg and leveled eyes of death at him. "My crew are missing. All of them. How is that possible? I thought this place had the best security around."

Forglyn smoothed his tie and gave a consoling look. "Relax, Glint. I've just been alerted. I'll have things in order soon."

"Well, nothing's been done so far. And this skrid here ..." I pointed to Grilg. "Only wanted to put one security detail on it."

Grilg took a step back, casting worried glances at us.

"Officer Grilg," Forglyn spoke in a measured tone with a subtle hint of scolding. "Place our ten best details on it immediately."

Grilg nodded quickly and began tapping away at his controls.

Forglyn looked at me. "I apologize, Glint. Let me handle this personally. Can we meet in your room?"

The thought of meeting that phony pretty boy face to face was appealing. My lizard fists and shiny new DEMOTER were close at hand. Something very exciting could happen. "You bet."

He nodded and the visual went blank. I shot a scowl at Grilg before heading out. I trudged past the front desk where the teen concierge was trying hard to avoid eye contact. On my way up to the room, several choice words rolled through my head for conversation starters.

I entered my room and caught sight of Forglyn standing by the full-length window. The sunlight was shimmering off his silver suit, giving him a radiant glow that I'm sure he was all too aware of.

My fingers danced across the handle of my pistol in anticipation. "So, where's my crew?"

Forglyn turned, his face filling with a smug grin. "I'm afraid they've all left, Captain."

I strode toward him, gripping the handle of my weapon. "Where?"

He shrugged. "Hard to say. Perhaps they grew tired of you … as I have."

There was a sharp prick in the back of my neck. I drew the DEMOTER and spun. A spherical droid hovered by the door, a thin barrel leveled at me. A quick squeeze of my trigger turned it into metal shards.

When I spun back to Forglyn, my movements weren't quite as smooth. I stumbled to my knees, gripping a nearby table for support. My vision was doubling. A shock of fear hit me that I was losing strength fast. I shook off the building haze and sent a barrage of DEMOTER fire his way. Several holo-shield tiles rose up before him, deflecting the blasts.

He shook his head. "The final stand of a dying space cowboy."

Despite all my rage and desperation, my body gave out. I slumped to the ground, the pistol falling from my grasp.

The blurry form of Forglyn stood over me. "You've had a great deal of luck to make it this far, Captain. But luck's not enough."

He was already my least favorite person in Glittronium but this was a whole new level. What angered me the most is that I never saw it coming. I struggled to maintain eye contact and promise retribution. "Yeeoo … rrghh … mlllth."

Forglyn kneeled close. "Easy Glint. It'll all be over soon. The last challenge starts in ten jemmins."

My brain begged my hands to reach out and choke the life out of him. Unfortunately, my body merely slumped to one side.

He chuckled. "Your performance in the challenge today should be enchanting. I can't wait." He gave me a few slaps on the cheek that I swore to avenge with DEMOTER blasts.

Forglyn stood and straightened his shiny suit. "I wouldn't worry about Jasette. She's safe with me." He grinned and strode out of the room.

CHAPTER 25

FAULTY FOOTING

THE NEXT FEW MOMENTS were a desperate struggle to crawl across the floor. Using every ounce of strength and determination, I only made it a few feet. My sad progress was another internal wound of defeat.

A blip sounded and the door opened.

Selinxia came rushing in. "Glint! What happened?"

"Glth ... mmff."

"Oh dear." She produced a miniature scanner and ran it over my forehead. "Drugged. Hmm. Someone's hedging their bets."

There was a pressurized sound and I felt a pinch at my neck.

"That should bring you around in a few jemmins," she said.

A prickly sensation went through my limbs. I still felt weak, but there was no doubt my condition was improving.

Selinxia glanced over her shoulder. "Someone's coming."

She disappeared into the sleeping chamber.

A squad of helmeted guards arrived at the door. They crowded around and lifted me up like a sack of wet clothes.

The next few moments were blurry. My arms were draped around two guards, who carried me down the hallway. After a head-spinning trip down the transverse cube, they marched me into the main room.

The visuals were bright and cataclysmic. Fiery comets were hurtling toward moons and crashing to the surface with violent impacts. Meteors composed of glow stones hurtled through space, smashing into each other in bright explosions of color.

The guards propped me up against an incline ramp and stood at either side of me.

"Look who's here." Forglyn's electronically enhanced voice boomed through the room.

He walked toward me, lit brightly with dozens of glow spheres. They circled around him like orbiting moons.

"Captain Glint Starcrost," he said. "The last of our final two contestants has finally arrived."

The crowd clapped and cheered.

"Let's hear it for our competitors, Chakdragonnon and Captain Starcrost." Forglyn waved his hand between me and the towering Vythian nearby.

Chak paced like a caged animal. In my hazy state, he seemed like a mountain of muscled scales and sharp teeth, ready to stamp me out of existence.

"Our competitors will face each other in lethal combat one last time," Forglyn said. "But only one will emerge as the Iron Gauntlet champion!"

The crowd stomped their feet in a thunderous response.

Forglyn turned to me. The bright spheres whirring around him made me dizzy.

"Are you ready for the final challenge?" A glowing,

audio orb weaved around Forglyn and stopped in front of me. It hovered in front of my mouth, waiting to amplify my response.

My mouth moved in slow motion. Something between a grunt and a stutter came out.

A devious smile spread across Forglyn's face. How badly I wanted to send my new scale-covered fist into his teeth. In a surge of anger I lunged toward him. Unfortunately, in my off condition, I fell forward, my fist taking a slow swing at empty air.

The guards lifted me, not kindly or carefully, back against the incline ramp.

"If you haven't noticed," Forglyn said. "The captain isn't feeling 100 percent today." He mimicked drinking a bottle and acting dizzy, soliciting laughter from the crowd. "But brave competitor that he is, he still wants to enter the challenge."

The crowd erupted in cheers.

"So, prepare yourself, because the final challenge of the Iron Gauntlet starts now!"

A bright light shone beneath me and the surge of teleportation energy carried me away.

CHAPTER 26

THE FINAL
CHALLENGE

I APPEARED on the frozen surface of a desolate, cold moon. Jagged formations of ice rose up all around, like crooked daggers. Dark chasms ribboned the landscape and white mountains loomed in the distance.

My breath came out in quick, white puffs of air. A gust of wind hit me like a swarm of frozen needles. I fumbled with my jacket for several cold moments until I was finally able to zip it up. The distant, electronic sounds of Forglyn and the crowd coming from my bracelet were lost in the harsh winds.

I hugged my arms for warmth. Whatever concoction Selinxia had given me was starting to normalize me. Plus, the mixture of cold and adrenaline was clearing my hazy state of mind. There was a bright flash in the distance, and Chak appeared on the snowy landscape in front of me. His facial scales were contorted with rage as he scanned the area. Finally, his eyes met mine and he arched back, letting loose a horrific Vythian howl.

Whenever Blix howled like that, it always inspired me,

teasing the notion that victory was at hand. Now that I was on the receiving end, it was far more terrifying.

The battle-ready Vythian charged toward me, snow kicking up behind him as he ran. The perfect blend of fear and panic sent me into a sprint in the opposite direction. I was still shaking off the drug effects, so my steps were a little squirrelly. My progress was more zig-zag than the beeline I hoped for.

All too soon the ragged breathing of an angry Vythian was closing in.

My heart was racing and the sharp, icy breaths felt like knives in my lungs. I was clearly outmatched on the brute strength level, but I still had a few tricks up my sleeve.

I looked back to see a wall of scaly muscles bearing down on me. His club was raised, ready to descend and smash my head into oblivion. I immediately collapsed into a tight ball on the ground. His foot slammed into my back, a painful but unavoidable effect of my tripping technique, and he sailed right over me.

I stood, watching him tumble through the snow in a flurry of white powder. I drew the DEMOTER X and sent a barrage of blasts into the white cloud. I knew it wouldn't do any serious damage, but it might mess him up enough to give me a good head start.

I ran toward a slanted tower of ice nearby that appeared to be the entrance to a cave. A narrow series of catacombs would be a great way to escape the clutches of a hulking foe. Sure, I might get lost forever in some underground maze, but I had to deal with the problem at hand.

The dreaded Vythian howl rang out behind me. There

was an extra layer of rage in the echoing tones. He'd recovered faster than I'd hoped, and he didn't sound happy.

I sprinted forward, trying to ignore the stabbing sensation in my lungs from the cold air. I neared the opening to the cave under the tower of ice. It was a dark unknown, but it was all I had to go with.

Behind me, through the snowy gusts of wind, I saw the dark shape of Chak heading toward me. He was still a ways off, but it wouldn't take him long to close the gap.

I surged forward, the cave just ahead. I hoped it burrowed underground away from the intense cold. I hoped it led to narrow passageways where an oversized Vythian couldn't follow me. I hoped for a great many things that were all dashed to bits as a towering, fang-filled monstrosity lumbered out of the cave.

Any remaining effects of the drug flew out of my body and took cover. I slid to a stop, gazing wide-eyed. The monster was almost as big as my star freighter. Thick, white fur covered his whole body except for a dark blue, apeish face. Angular black eyes glared down at me, the unluckiest of intruders. His cavernous maw was filled with giant fangs that made me want to cry. The beast let loose a thunderous roar that put the Vythian howl to shame.

Panic took over strategy and any logic whatsoever. I ran like a crazy person in the opposite direction.

Chak was dead ahead. He was frozen in place, staring at the monster behind me with a worried expression. If that beast was enough to strike fear into the heart of a Vythian, I wanted to be far away from this place.

I ran past him at full speed, not bothering to look back. The ground began to tremble as the huge snow beast thundered after me. My chances of survival were dwindling fast, and the only panic-driven solution going through my head was to run like mad.

Chancing a look behind, I saw Chak facing off against the behemoth. I felt a surge of admiration at the bravery of Vythian kind, but the moment didn't last long. The towering creature swatted Chak away like a pesky fly.

Much to my dismay, the snow beast looked back toward me and resumed his pursuit.

Suddenly, a bright thought hit me like a ray of sunshine. I had *wings*. I could simply fly away. In all the panic, I'd forgotten. My heart soared and I took to the air. The ascent was a rush of cold, the fear prompting my wings to beat faster. The wind grew increasingly violent as I rose, and I found it difficult to fly in one direction as the strong gusts of cold air buffeted me about.

The snow beast closed the distance at an alarming rate, let out an enraged roar and—to my horror—leapt toward me with outstretched hands.

His leaping ability was terrifying for his size and quickly wiped away any hope I had left. A furry hand the size of a shuttle craft swung toward me. In that brief moment of reaction time, I tried to fly away, and I was almost successful. But a thick finger grazed my back and sent me spinning through the air.

For a few moments, all I could do was gasp to catch my breath and let the strong winds take me. After a few harrowing freems of tumbling through the icy air, I landed in a soft hill of snow.

I thrashed about until my head and arms broke through the surface. I was waist deep in the powder. The winds picked up and I was all squints, trying to look around. There was a dull pain in my back sending evil little pulses of agony shooting up my neck. A few labored steps through the thick snow made minimal progress, so it was time to take flight again.

A strong thrust of my wings filled my back with searing pain. As I stood there wincing, waiting for the icy cold to numb the agony, I vowed not to use my wings for the rest of the day. Getting hit by the snow beast must've tweaked them pretty bad. I couldn't crane my head back far enough to see the amount of damage, but judging by the pain it had to be pretty extensive.

The ground beneath me started to tremble. There was only one logical reason for it. There was no flying away this time. I froze, hoping he would pass by unaware. As his massive frame emerged directly ahead and his dark eyes locked onto me, I knew I'd have no such luck.

CHAPTER 27

AN ICY SLIDE

THE SNOW BEAST took a step toward me, his apish face contorting with malice. A loud crack came from beneath me and the ground shifted. The beast froze for a moment, a worried look on his face. I was just thinking how strange it was for a creature of his size to worry and how foreign that expression must've been to his face when the ground opened up beneath us.

There was a terrifying drop of weightlessness. The powder fell alongside me like a great snowfall. I hit an icy slope and soon I was sliding down a huge, frozen tunnel.

The tunnel shook with thunderous impact as the snow beast thrashed about behind me. His colossal roar echoed off the tunnel walls as we continued down in an uncontrolled slide.

The tunnel had a luminous, light blue property that bathed the area in an ethereal light. I would've been impressed by the sight if I wasn't careening helplessly along with an angry behemoth close behind.

There was a smaller tunnel branching off up ahead. It

was coming up quickly, so I wasted little time angling my body toward it. My body drifted closer but not enough. I was going to miss it. Strange as it felt, I extended the claws on my new lizard-like hands and dug them into the ice. I lost a precious few moments adjusting them to steer my descent in the right direction but in the end, I was heading straight for the smaller tunnel.

I plunged into the tunnel, filled with relief at the sight of the snow beast sliding down the opposite tunnel. The new tunnel was a gentler slope but it curved constantly like the path of a drunken snake. There were several moments of painful zigzagging before I was unceremoniously dumped onto a level surface.

I struggled to a sitting position, feeling the sharp pangs of fresh bruises and battered wings. It took a few moments to catch my breath, looking in wonder at my new surroundings: a circular room of the luminous blue ice, the walls well fashioned, smooth and symmetrical. The room was several times the size of my luxury suite, and a few arched passageways branched off from it.

By far, the strangest sight in the room was just a few steps away. Standing there, holding a glittering necklace, stood an ice statue of Forglyn Sashmeyer.

The carving was so detailed I had to resist the impulse to blast it into ice chips. The statue held the necklace as if offering it to me. It was none other than the final Iron Gauntlet.

I got up and headed closer. DEMOTER in hand, I made a slow sweep of the other passageways in case anything was lurking, waiting to leap out and attack.

The statue stood directly before me. The glint of steel from the Iron Gauntlet necklace winked at me as it hung from Forglyn's open hand. It was hard to believe my wild change of fortune—not only had I survived the competition but victory was right in front of me. All I had to do was reach out and take it. I tapped at my chest, giving subtle acknowledgement to the Emerald Enigma lying hidden under my shirt.

I reached for the necklace.

"Not so fast." The statue said.

I took a step back, leveling my pistol at the statue's head.

A sim projection animated the face of the statue, making it look alive.

"You didn't think it would be this easy, did you?" The statue said.

"You call what I just went through easy?" I said.

Sections of the floor fell away and dozens of Forglyn statues rose up throughout the room. Each one held an identical Iron Gauntlet necklace. Soon the room was filled. There had to be around a hundred statues to choose from.

"Choose wisely, Iron Gauntlet competitor," the statue said. "The wrong choice can prove … regrettable."

The sim face projection disappeared. I was left with rows of smiling ice Forglyns daring me to make the wrong choice.

Since this was the last challenge, I wasn't taking any chances. No impulsive decisions. I would do a thorough search of the room before touching a thing.

An echoing sound of footsteps came from one of the arched passages. Chak charged into the room and slid to a stop. He spotted me and his face contorted with malice. He leveled his mace at me. "I will crush your puny—"

His rant ceased when he caught sight of the necklaces. A cruel smile spread across his face. With a guttural yell, he lunged for the necklace on the closest statue. An electric crackling filled the room and a jagged blue energy flowed around the Vythian. His body convulsed for a few moments before he dropped to his knees.

I stared in horror at the myriad of statues before me, waiting to inflict similar pain. If they could send a Vythian to his knees, I didn't want any part of it. Chak groaned and struggled to his feet. He hissed at the statue before him and swung his club. The club connected with the icy head, smashing it into a million ice fragments.

To my surprise, Chak grabbed for the necklace on the next statue. Another jolt of blue energy hit him. He cried out and fell to his side. Obviously, pain wasn't a major problem for him.

My mind raced for a way out of this. All the statues and necklaces looked identical. I didn't know how many wrong choices I could survive.

Chak swayed as he regained footing. "I can take the pain until I be holding the last Gauntlet." He stabilized and stared me down. "I doubt ye can handle the same. But just to be sure."

He raised his mace and charged me. Without thinking, I dodged through the narrow spaces between statues. A spray of ice hit my back as Chak smashed the statue behind me. I glanced back, watching him pulverize the bottom half of the statue.

I threaded a careful path through a few rows of icy Forglyns. Thankfully, they were close enough together to make a large, armor-clad Vythian's progress far more difficult. There was an electric crackling and I spun around. A necklace had touched Chak's mace, sending another shock through him. He was on one knee, breathing heavily.

A moment of pleasure at his mistake distracted me just enough to make a careless move. As I turned back around, the corner of my jacket hit a necklace.

I watched, in slow motion it seemed, as a bright blue current flowed from the necklace into my jacket. A shock of pain hit me. My bones felt like they were on fire. I collapsed to the floor between two statues, crying out from the pain. The electric current continued to flow through me, sending my muscles into uncontrollable spasms.

The room spun and I felt myself sliding from consciousness. My body wanted to let go and pass out. I fought against it with every ounce of strength. If I blacked out, I knew that would be the end of me.

My mind focused on Jasette. I had to stay alert if there was any chance of seeing her again.

I rolled to my back, still convulsing with the electrical energy. A spray of ice hit me. Looking up, I saw the looming, copper-scaled Vythian. He gave a powerful sweep of his mace, obliterating the only statue that stood between us. My body wasn't responding correctly. Muscle spasms made every movement jerky and unpredictable. I tried to slide backward through the statues on either side of me. I only made it halfway before the Vythian stood at my feet.

Chak glared down at me. "Now you die, human pest."

He raised his mace for a final strike. The statues eft a nice open path for his mace to pass through before it crushed me.

There was time for one last move. Out of instinct, I drew my DEMOTER. My hand was shaky, but I could still aim in his general direction. I sent a wild spray of blasts at the legs of the statues on either side of me.

One of the statues angled inward and toppled the surprised Vythian. He cried out in a rage as it knocked him down.

My blasts were far from accurate, and I wasn't as lucky with the other statue. It cracked and fell backward toward me. A descending elbow just missed my head as it shattered on the floor. My eyes widened as a glittering necklace draped over my leg. I winced and prepared for the searing jolt of pain.

A surge of energy hit me, but to my surprise there was no pain. Everything went bright white. There was a soft popping in my ears, and the next sound I heard was a cheering crowd of Iron Gauntlet fans.

"Glint Starcrost." Forglyn's amplified voice echoed throughout the main room in Shansmannor hall. His usual confidence and smooth oratory skills were gone. There was a noticeable tremble in his voice. "It looks like the game is over. And … there's our winner."

The crowd hooted and cheered. I was having trouble connecting the sights with reality. Had I really made it back? Did I just win the insane contest known as the Iron Gauntlet?

I was still on my back, trying to gain control of my spasming muscles. Guards circled around, lifting me to my feet.

Forglyn stepped close, his eyes dark and serious. "How do you feel, Captain? Luck must be on your side." His jaw muscles rippled like he was grinding his teeth. "Outclassed by superior contestants, somehow you stumbled to victory in the Iron Gauntlet."

I gripped the handle of the DEMOTER. A large guard with a unibrow grabbed my arm and gave a grim shake of his head. I stared down Forglyn. "Where's Jasette?"

"I'm afraid you'll have to deal with relationship issues on your own." He cast a playful look at the crowd as if sharing an inside joke. The crowd laughed in response.

"As you all know, several attempts were made to break into the Iron Gauntlet vault." Forglyn said. "But as always, our superior security prevailed. Many Glittronium treasures are locked in that vault, including this …"

Forglyn motioned to two slinky blonde women dressed in sequined, black gowns. They sauntered toward me, directing a hovering black case almost their height. A glowing green Iron Gauntlet symbol pulsated on the front of the case.

"Here is your prize." Forglyn struggled to keep a smile on his face. "One million vibes."

One of the blondes opened the case. The bright green glow of vibe cubes shone forth. The crowd cheered at the sight.

I'd rarely seen a vibe cube in person, much less a chest filled with them. They were the most concentrated form of vibe energy. Each cube was worth ten thousand common street vibes.

"Well, that does it." Forglyn said. "Let's give a final hand to this season's winner of the Iron Gauntlet."

The applause of the crowd filled the room.

Forglyn moved aside his glowing audio sphere and gave me an icy look. "This isn't over, Glint." He turned and stormed out of the room.

If my limbs were in normal working order, I would've charged after him. As it was, I had to let the guards half carry me back to my room.

• • •

"Congratulations, Captain." Jenson's voice was filled with excitement as the guards helped me through the door of my luxury suite. "I knew you would emerge victorious. I simply knew it."

The guards dropped me unceremoniously on a pile of silken pillows. The two blonde women left the black case filled with vibe squares hovering near my feet. They smiled, blew me a kiss, then sashayed out of the room.

The bulky guards followed close behind. As they headed for the door, the guard with a unibrow turned and placed my DEMOTER on the entry table.

"Be careful with that." The guard spoke as if daring me. "We'll be right outside."

The door closed and I took a deep breath, my head still spinning from recent events.

"I must say," Jenson said. "I've never had the privilege of hosting an Iron Gauntlet champion in my room. This is quite an honor."

I was definitely going to miss Jenson. "Any word on my crew?"

"No, sir. Terribly sorry."

I had to find Forglyn. I'd wring his neck until he told me what he did with Jasette.

I attempted to stand. My knees buckled and I fell against a low table. After a few moments of struggling, I was on my knees, leaning against the table for support.

The door to my room dematerialized and Selinxia stood there. A sparkling, silver body suit accentuated her curvy frame. She was beaming, and her arms were all jittery as if she was trying to keep from jumping up and down.

The guard leaned his head in. "She okay?"

I nodded and the guard motioned her in. The door rematerialized behind her and she let loose a yelp of victory.

"You did it, Glint. You actually did it!" She moved across the room like an excited butterfly and huddled next to me.

She grabbed my arm, looking concerned. "Are you okay?"

"I'm fine." I tried to stand but my legs weren't cooperating.

Selinxia held me as I slumped back to my knees. "Take it easy, Glint. You've had a long day." She turned my face to her. "Don't worry, I'll take care of you."

She got up and headed to the room computer panel. Her fingers danced across the controls.

"Selinxia, I hate to interrupt," Jenson said. "But the override controls you're entering are in direct violation of—"

Jenson's voice trailed off into a series of descending blips. There was a sluggish whir of several systems powering down.

"What are you doing?" I said.

She turned, a playful smile on her face. "I just wanted a moment alone before I said goodbye." Selinxia moved close and knelt down so we were face to face. "You know, we don't have to say goodbye. Come with me, Glint."

My mind locked for a moment. This new layer of confusion was just too much to handle.

"What?" I finally managed. "Where?"

She shook her head and smiled. "Anywhere."

"But my crew is—"

"Your crew is gone." She put her hand on my shoulder. "I'm sorry, Glint, but obviously someone wanted you out of the competition. I knew that when I found you drugged in your room. It's clear they got rid of your crew first. This competition brings out some ruthless characters."

"No." I tried to stand but my legs gave out once more.

She steadied me and stroked my face. "I know it's hard. It'll take time to accept. I can promise you this much, I'll be with you through it all. We'll start a new crew. With your winnings, you can hire any crew you want."

For a moment I imagined flying away with Selinxia. No doubt my prize money could afford an incredible new starship and a crack team of crewmembers. A few gloons ago, before I met my crew, it was the sort of thing I'd dreamed about.

Selinxia grabbed my hands. "What do you say?"

Her bright blue eyes looked into mine, promising a new start. But as beautiful as she was and as sleek and deadly as my new ship and crew appeared in my imagination, it all seemed hollow. I couldn't leave without Jasette, Blix, and even Nelvan. As strange as it was to admit, they were the closest thing to a family I had. If there was even the slightest chance that they might be alive somewhere, I had to search for them.

"I can't," I said. "You're great and everything, but I can't leave without my crew."

She paused for a moment, then gave a knowing nod. "You know, there are a lot of space drifters out there that would've taken me up on that offer."

I shrugged. "I suppose so."

"I guess that's why I'm going to let you live."

There was a sharp prick at my wrist and my body went limp. I slumped over on the pillows nearby.

CHAPTER 28

REVENGE

I LAY ON THE PILLOWS, feeling paralyzed. My mouth moved like I was talking underwater. "What did you do?"

"I'm sorry, Glint. I hate to drug you but in all fairness, I did counteract Forglyn's drug earlier, so really, I'm just putting you back to where you were."

"You can't ... my crew." My tongue felt swollen.

Selinxia stood and strode toward the black hover chest. She ran her hand along the glowing Iron Gauntlet symbol. "You really defied all my expectations, you know." A ripple moved through her skin. "I'd hoped you'd make it through at least one, maybe two challenges and give me some time to break into the Gauntlet vault." Her skin changed to a silver color. "But you go and win the whole blasted Iron Gauntlet." Scales formed on her skin and her bone structure shifted until she took the form of Silvet, the snakey messenger of Parallax.

"Silvet?" My lips felt numb as I spoke. "It's been you the whole time?"

"How else could I keep an eye on you?" Her voice lacked

the hissing, raspy tones as it did when we first met. It even differed from the bubbly, excited sound of Selinxia. Now it had the smooth, rich cadence of a confident woman. "I put the real Selinxia on a resort shuttle to the tropical moons of Fendillis. After a potent memory drug, she's blissfully unaware of the concierge job on Glittronium she was supposed to show up for."

Silvet opened the chest, the green glow of vibe bars illuminating her silver face. She lifted one of the bars high, her blue eyes drinking it in. "The life of a thief can be difficult, but it's moments like these that make it all worthwhile."

"What about Parallax?" I spoke with effort. "We had a deal."

Silvet grinned. "I made him up. Along with my friends here." She activated a thin bracelet on her wrist and a host of dark wraiths floated around her. "Realistic simulations, don't you think?"

I scowled at the floating wraiths, feeling my anger rise.

"Please don't be upset," she said. "The deal was my only way of keeping you in the competition until I could break into the vault. We thieves need a flair for the theatrical now and then. Unfortunately, their security proved more difficult than I'd hoped. But in the end, it didn't matter. You brought the treasure right to me." She winked.

"You'll ... pay ... for ... this." It took every ounce of my fading strength to threaten her.

A sad look crossed her face. "Oh now, don't be like that. I tell you what ..." She went to the entry table and retrieved my DEMOTER X. Soon she was back at my side. "I look at us as partners in this little caper." She re-holstered my pistol and slid a vibe bar in the inner pocket of my kandrelian hide jacket. "Consider this your cut."

As wildly unfair as my "cut" of the money was when, after all, I'd done all the hard work, my mouth refused to utter the threats and curses churning through my head. The only response I could manage was to glare at her.

She gave me a kiss on the cheek and stood. Her body morphed once more, and within moments she'd turned into an exact replica of me.

"Well, I guess I'd better get going." She spoke with my lower, rough voice. "No hard feelings?" She smiled my own smile back at me.

My vision started to blur. I felt myself slipping from consciousness.

She placed a few pillows over me to hide me from sight. Through a gap in the pillows, I could still see the room. The last thing I saw before everything went black was the clone of me leading the black hover case filled with vibes toward the door.

I awoke to the soft orange glow of a holding cylinder. The orange energy held me firmly in place. Judging by the stylish construction and the advanced holoscreen controls, I was in a luxury space cruiser.

Forglyn walked into the room, hands clasped loosely behind his back. "Finally awake, are we?" He flashed a confident smirk and strode toward me.

"You filthy skrid." I gave him a dark look. "What is this? Where's Jasette?"

"Don't worry. Soon you won't have anything left to worry

about." He cast a bemused look at me. "I still can't believe you won. A worthless, uncouth space cowboy." His face tightened with anger. "You made my investors very unhappy."

"Good. Maybe they'll blast you into oblivion."

He wagged a correcting finger at me. "No, no. You're the one who caused the problem. It is you who will be dealt with."

A tall, thin man in a white coat came into the room with a hover tray in tow. The tray was filled with sharp looking surgical laser tools.

"This is Doctor Klonstrik." Forglyn motioned to the thin man. "My personal plastic surgeon."

The doctor brought the hover tray next to my holding cylinder. His cold, grey eyes swept over my body as he made adjustments to a glowing, hook-shaped tool.

"There was a report that you left right after the competition," Forglyn said. "Prize money and all. Rumor had it you disabled my guards and left in some fast, cloak-enabled space cruiser. I sent several ships in pursuit and came up empty. I must say, I was taken off guard. I thought for a moment you'd bested me." He chuckled. "Then I find you unconscious in your room." He gave an apologetic look. "How sad. Your crew lost, your riches stolen away only moments after victory. I suppose you're destined to remain a poor, lonely space drifter."

I gritted my teeth and stared at him in fury. "That just means I've got nothing to lose. I won the Iron Gauntlet and my next mission is to take you out of your cushy, little life and knock you into the gutters of the universe."

Forglyn smiled and shook his head. "Delusions, Captain. Sad delusions."

The doctor watched me with lifeless eyes and raised his glowing tool. "Shall we begin?"

Forglyn nodded and took a step back to allow the doctor room. "Well, Glint, you gave me nothing but grief this season of the competition."

The doctor activated the controls on my holding cylinder. It slowly lowered to a horizontal position.

"Frankly, I don't know how you survived," Forglyn continued. "But I'm guessing it had something to do with these ... unique physical traits of yours." He motioned to my hands and wings.

The doctor and Forglyn stood over me. Forglyn nodded at the doctor as if to prompt whatever horrible process was about to begin. I struggled against the energy field but it was hopeless. I was held firmly in place.

The doctor activated another control on the holding cylinder and a foul smelling mist washed over me. I felt my consciousness slipping away.

Forglyn leaned over me. "I decided, as punishment for the trouble you caused me, to take away everything that makes you ... special."

My last sight as I slipped away was the doctor's tool-filled hands moving toward me.

A sleepy feeling hung over me as I passed an endless row of beautiful women. They stood motionless in the shallow recesses of a towering wall fashioned with large, black stones. Each woman I passed seemed to awaken at my approach and stare unblinking with glowing, white eyes. They all wore the same outfit. A charcoal grey, fitted jumpsuit with an oval red symbol on their chest.

I was gliding forward, fastened to an upright hover platform. Forglyn walked on one side of me. To my horror, the evil cyborg that I'd thought long dead walked along on the other side. His metal body was scarred and pitted. It was a small consolation, but at least the river serpent had done some damage before he escaped.

Several hover crates moved alongside them as we headed down a cavernous castle hallway. The hall was flanked by endless rows of the statue-like women.

There was no escaping the awful truth of my predicament. I was in none other than Mar Mar the Unthinkable's castle. Aside from his loyal minions, few made it out of Mar Mar's castle alive—or at least undamaged.

I'd met the powerful gangster once, several gloons ago, as part of a team of smugglers I immediately regretted teaming up with. They had botched our mission and we'd returned to Mar Mar with half the promised payment. Our team of smugglers entered twelve strong and left two weak. Myself and the other rookie on the team were let go because, as Mar Mar put it, "we weren't complete fools."

I found out soon after that he'd placed a one hundred vibe bounty on my head. It was a lesser bounty, but enough to make my life edgy for the next few gloons. Recently however, it had been upgraded to fifty thousand vibes. There really was no reason for the wild upswing in price that I could figure out. I hadn't seen him since that fateful day when I barely escaped this place. I guess I was about to find out.

"Gleeeent." The cyborg looked over at me, the cavity in his helmet glowing red. "Mar Mar's prize. Time to cooooollect."

"Good, you're awake," Forglyn smiled. "Welcome to Mar Mar's castle. As my most valued investor, I'm bringing him double his wager and throwing you in as a bonus."

I suddenly remembered his doctor and the surgical nightmare that transpired while I was out. I looked down and was relieved to find all my limbs intact. My usual star pilot outfit was on and I saw no large gashes or dripping blood. So far so good.

I was secured to the hover platform with metal clasps. A thrill went through me at the sight of regular hands. No more lizard scales or claws. My good old human hands were back.

"Behold your mediocrity." Forglyn announced. "Gone are your special wings and dangerous hands. You're just a normal human like the rest of us now."

He broke into a mocking laugh. The fact that he'd done me the biggest favor in the universe was completely lost on him. I was myself again. No more freakish parts. Although, if I was being completely honest, I would miss the freedom of flight.

"How does it feel, Glint?" Forglyn fixed me with cruel eyes.

I shrugged. "I'm fine with it."

The wind seemed to go out of his sails. He seemed confused for a moment, before his confident sneer returned. "Sure you are. Don't play tough with me. I know your spirit is crushed. No more wings, no more claws. All you have left is some worthless, green necklace that we couldn't remove. A curse you were shackled with from a lost bet, no doubt."

I kept my poker face intact, but inside I was doing back flips. I was a normal human again, and he had no clue my necklace was the legendary Emerald Enigma. "Something like that."

"I figured as much. Space drifters like you pick up a lot of trash along the way." Forglyn smirked and looked ahead. "There it is. Mar Mar's throne room."

A broad arch at the end of the hallway opened to a spacious room ahead. Everything in the room appeared to be either fashioned from precious jewels or encrusted with them. Man-sized diamond insets framed the archway.

My fate was sealed. "Since I'm gonna die anyways, I have to know. Who is this cyborg and why won't he die?"

Forglyn cast an amused look at the cyborg. "Frankly, I was hoping you'd tell me. He's one of Mar Mar's new bounty hunters. Once you were picked as a contestant, Mar Mar said he had a new hunter dead set on capturing you. Some old vendetta or something. I sent him after you in a few of the challenges. Unfortunately, you escaped. He calls himself Mishdrone."

"Mishdrone?" There was something sickeningly familiar about that name. I flashed back to a recent memory of my old nemesis, Hamilton Von Drone and his robot Mishmash struggling to crawl out of the lava caverns. The explosion from my old DEMOTER and the lava must have fused them together in some bizarre amalgam.

The cyborg was looking at me. The red band in his helmet was pulsating with light.

"Mishdrone." I spoke the new name aloud as if it were a dark spell.

A panel slid open in Mishdrone's side. He reached in and pulled out my DEMOTER X. He pointed it at my head, pretended to fire, then emitted a strange, repeating, screeching sound as he returned my pistol to his side. My guess was that it was a cyborg taunt of some kind.

Mishdrone pointed to the throne room dead ahead and made a fist. This was his moment of victory.

Several fembots peeled away from their frozen stances in the hallway and walked alongside us as we entered Mar Mar's dreaded throne room.

CHAPTER 29

MAR MAR
IS DISPLEASED

THE BROAD, diamond-framed archway ushered us into a grand room of opulence. Mar Mar had a taste for the décor of ancient rulers of legend; monuments of wood and stone framed the sparkling room. There were random piles of gemstones and racks of finely crafted weaponry, but the main constant of the room was a series of Mar Mar statues in various poses of power. Plenty of flexing and outstretched arms of victory as foes lay vanquished beneath his feet. It was completely excessive, exceedingly prideful, and—unfortunately—mostly true. He was the most powerful gangster in the known universe.

Of course, all the sparkles and shiny coatings were just the surface ornaments. The true underpinnings and power of his kingdom were driven by the most advanced and dangerous technology money could buy.

We approached a giant, black metal throne decked out in artistic patterns of glittering jewels. Mar Mar reclined on his throne. He wore his signature black leather armor that exposed his powerful arms and legs. A black iron crown accented with a dark ruby sat atop his broad, grey head.

He was flanked by several beautiful fembots. They stood at attention, their glowing white eyes staring dead ahead and their dual red laser swords drawn and crossed before them. Even at their height of six foot plus, they looked like children next to Mar Mar.

He let out a low grunt at our arrival and shifted his husky, grey body to a more alert posture. A long handled, double-bladed axe lay across his throne. He held the handle in a relaxed manner, rolling it slowly along the dark armrests causing the double blade to spin and showcase the razor-sharp edges.

"Forglyn." Mar Mar's low, resonant voice called out. "Is this the splinter in my finger?"

"Indeed." Forglyn bowed. "As promised, I've brought you the returns on your wager and this troublesome human to do with as you like." Mishdrone brought the long hover crates to the foot of the throne. The lids slid open to reveal countless, glowing vibe bars within. Mar Mar frowned. "Is that all?"

Forglyn's ever-cocky composure was replaced with lines of concern. "That's double your wager. A generous return if you ask me."

"I'd expected four times the amount for my trouble." Mar Mar gave a displeased look.

"Four?" Forglyn gave a nervous chuckle. "That's crazy."

Mar Mar narrowed his gaze. "What did you call me?"

"Nothing, nothing." All of Forglyn's confidence vanished. His nervous eyes darted around at the armed fembots around us. "It's just ... four times, I mean, that will—"

"Slow your expansion of power?" Mar Mar watched him intently.

Forglyn paused. It looked like he was having trouble forming words.

"You think I don't know about your plans?" Mar Mar continued. "Takeovers of vulnerable planets, exploiting your celebrity influence ... attempting to rival my power."

"No, never!" Forglyn was starting to panic. "I just ... I only want a little power. I would never rival you."

"You're right about that." Mar Mar brought the long hilt of his axe to the floor, creating a resounding thud. Fembots stealthily moved into formation around Forglyn.

"Mar Mar, please!" Forglyn pleaded. "I beg of you—"

"Silence." Mar Mar said.

I was filled with happiness and butterflies at Forglyn's groveling demise. It took all my strength to hold back the laughter at this turn of events. I felt downright giddy until Mar Mar turned his attention to me.

Mar Mar signaled to the nearby fembots. They undid the metal clasps, and I slid to my feet. I stood there rubbing my wrists, sore from the tight clasps, and feeling a little more confident now that I wasn't tied down anymore.

"As for you, Glint Starcrost." Mar Mar's cold eyes bored into me. "What have you to say for your crimes against my good pleasure?"

It was said there were no good answers to Mar Mar's questions. Since it was a losing game anyway, I decided to answer on my own terms. It was time to go out fighting like a real space captain.

I squared my shoulders. "I'm the winner of the Iron Gauntlet. This bounty hunter tried to ruin my victory." I pointed at Mishdrone. "If Forglyn is telling you how to bet your money, he should've known I'd be the one to bet on. It was his bad advice that caused you all the grief. Without these two skrids getting in the way, you could've bet on me and won all the vibes without any of the hassle. These two are the real splinters in your finger."

Mar Mar leaned back in his throne, a thoughtful look on his grim face. "An interesting point."

"What?" Forglyn looked somewhere between desperation and rage. "You're actually listening to this fool?"

Mar Mar leaned forward, looking stern. "Are you calling my contemplations foolish?"

"No, of course not." Forglyn waved his hands as if to wipe away his own words.

"The time has come." Mar Mar stood, his impressive, twelve-foot stature making me feel nervous and twitchy. His tall handled axe was clutched firmly in his hand, matching his height.

"Wait." Forglyn held up his hands as if a flood was about to descend on him. "I'll give you four times the amount. Five times!"

Mar Mar marched down the black staircase, the nearby fembots falling in line behind him. All too soon he stood before us.

He lifted his axe above us, alternating it between Forglyn and myself.

"I am displeased." He spoke matter-of-factly.

"Mar Mar is displeased." The fembots echoed his statement in perfect unison.

"Someone must pay for my displeasure," he said.

"Someone must pay for Mar Mar's displeasure," the fembots repeated.

He leveled the axe over Forglyn's head. "What can you offer as appeasement for my wrath?"

"I'll pay you eight times the amount." Forglyn was trembling, staring wide-eyed at the axe. "Ten times!"

Mar Mar moved the axe over my head. "What can you offer as appeasement for my wrath?"

I was definitely outmatched on appeasement offerings. Forglyn was rich; I was broke. A broken-down star freighter and a humble amount of vibes couldn't stand against vast celebrity wealth. I was about to weave a tale of hidden treasure on a distant moon that Mar Mar would never believe when a bright thought hit me like a DEMOTER blast.

"Have you ever heard of the Emerald Enigma?" I said.

Mar Mar's eyebrow raised. "I've heard the legend."

"Then you know of its power?"

He grinned. "I know the tales. What are you getting at?"

I paused for dramatic emphasis. "The Emerald Enigma is more than a tale. It's a powerful talisman and I'm offering it to you now as appeasement." I pulled the green gemstone from under my shirt and let it hang from my neck, enticing his curiosity.

A sharp sound like the screeching of metal came from Mishdrone. He turned toward me and clamped his thick, metal hands around my throat. Mar Mar brought the flat of his axe down on Mishdrone's head, making a loud, clanking sound. The red light in Mishdrone's head went dim and he crumpled to the floor.

Mar Mar shook his head. "Bounty hunters. What a freakish lot." He bent down, narrowing his eyes at the Enigma.

"It's a lie," Forglyn said. "That's not the real Enigma. It can't be."

Mar Mar motioned toward Forglyn with the axe. "Silence."

Forglyn held his tongue with difficulty. He looked like he was having trouble staying still.

Mar Mar examined the green gemstone a moment longer, then straightened, leaning his long-handled axe against his shoulder. His attention shifted toward a reinforced steel door in the side of the room. "Oracle. Come forth."

The steel door slid open. A pyramid-shaped silver droid about my size hovered out of it. Rings of multicolored lights blinked across its surface. It hovered over to Mar Mar and stopped.

Mar Mar turned to me, a bemused look on his face. "Now then, Glint Starcrost, bringer of legends. Convince me of your veracity."

I was in too far now. I decided to lay it all out there. "How do you think I was able to survive and win the Iron Gauntlet? How is it possible I beat out all those powerful competitors? I'm just a human. An out-of-work space captain. My skills are mediocre at best."

As much as I hated understating my awesomeness, I had to play it humble to make a strong case.

Mar Mar looked at the Oracle droid. The lights blinked rapidly across its silver surface and a quick series of beeps sounded.

Mar Mar turned back to me. "Continue."

I prepared for another round. "I was given the Enigma by a man named Grizzolo. Another human who miraculously survived a previous Iron Gauntlet and almost won."

Mar Mar checked the droid again and nodded. "Your odds are improving by the freem."

"What?" Forglyn sounded exasperated. "This is crazy. You can't really believe that dingy little stone is the Enigma." Forglyn pointed a shaky finger at the small stone around my neck.

Mar Mar gave Forglyn a dark look.

Since the scales were weighing in my favor, I decided to add more to the pile. "Plus, the Iron Gauntlet super computer picked me. Out of all the powerful creatures in the universe, why would it pick me … unless I wore the powerful talisman known as the Emerald Enigma?"

Mar Mar nodded, as if persuaded. "Quite true."

Forglyn was taking quick, nervous breaths, like he was hyperventilating. "A computer glitch. Computers are faulty. They make mistakes all the time."

The Oracle droid made a sharp, beeping sound.

Mar Mar glanced down at the droid. "Quite right, Oracle. Quite right." He lifted his axe above Forglyn.

"No!" Forglyn pleaded. "I beg you!"

"I have made my choice." Mar Mar wore a grim face.

"Mar Mar has chosen," the fembots repeated.

He narrowed his eyes at Forglyn. "Take him to the dungeons."

Several fembots grabbed Forglyn and dragged him from the room. Hearing his fading shouts of protest and promised vengeance were like a beautiful symphony.

Mar Mar turned his attention back to me. "Oracle calculates a ninety two percent chance the amulet you wear is the authentic Emerald Enigma." He held out his thick hand. "Relinquish it to me now."

This was the tricky part where my whole gamble could come crashing down. I had to play upon his delusions of royalty. "Mar Mar, your power and wealth are unmatched. It would be my honor to give you this legendary object."

Mar Mar gave a slight nod, as if acknowledging something fairly obvious. He flicked the fingers of his open hand toward him as if to prompt my delivery of the necklace. Only one obstacle remained. I had to get him to agree to accept the accursed thing before I could get it off my neck. Anything short of that would cause it to constrict around my neck and raise suspicions.

I continued with my regal babblings. "Oh great and wise Mar Mar, all your ways are just and fair. Let me be a humble servant and present it to you with the ceremony fit for a mighty king." The words weren't perfect but it was good enough, for a last ditch effort.

Mar Mar sighed and gave a wave of his hand. "Very well. Make it quick."

I grabbed the necklace and gave a theatrical bow. "Mar Mar, strong and wise, will you agree to bear the Emerald Enigma?"

"Yes, lowly insect. Now give it to me."

I could see he was losing patience, but I had to press my luck. "Oh large and grey one, any servant who would ask you to lift a finger should be slain. Work and toil should be left for slaves, not for your impressiveness. Please allow me the privilege of placing it over your royal head."

Mar Mar paused in thought for several terrifying moments. "Very well."

He removed his heavy, iron crown and leaned toward me, his eyes watching me closely. Several fembots rushed closer, their glowing laser swords drawn and poised inches away from my neck.

I lifted the necklace, slow and cautious. My heart raced as it slid over my head without constricting. I carefully placed it over his thick head. The necklace instantly loosened to account for his immense skull and slid down to his neck like a deadly asp waiting for the right moment to strike.

A thrill of hope shot through me. I strained to keep my expression blank, even though I wanted to leap up and shout for joy.

Mishdrone stirred and with a clumsy, clanking of metal on the stone floor, he got back to his feet. The red band of light on his head grew bright as he watched the Enigma hanging from Mar Mar's neck.

Mar Mar straightened, a curious look on his face. "I can feel the sensation of power." He gave a wicked grin. "This must be the Emerald Enigma indeed."

I gave a sad nod, as though I'd lost a fortune in a card game. "Yes. I hate to give up such a treasure, but if it saves my life and takes the bounty off my head, it's what I have to do."

Mar Mar smirked. "You press your luck, Starcrost."

Blast. I went too far with the bounty request.

"I admit, you have found some favor with me." He held the green stone before him in admiration. I cringed, praying he wouldn't try to lift it any higher. "But not very long ago, I raised your bounty to fifty thousand vibes for a reason."

Although I didn't want to remind him of his anger, I just had to know. "Why?"

He paused for a moment, looking thoughtful. "I don't remember."

How could I argue with that logic? "Well, since I gave you the Enigma, couldn't we call it even?"

He gave a slow shake of his head. "No."

"Um, okay. How about lowering it?"

He rubbed his chin. "Fine. Oracle, adjust Glint Starcrost's bounty to five hundred vibes."

The Oracle droid emitted a string of beeps and his lights seemed to move faster for a moment.

Five hundred wasn't ideal, but it was better than fifty thousand. "Thank you, your highness. Can I … I mean, if there's nothing else … can I go now?"

"Go?" Mar Mar chuckled. "No one just walks out of my castle that easily after causing grief." He aimed his axe at Mishdrone. "Bounty hunter, take Starcrost to the upper prisons." He turned to me. "The food is decent, and you get a small window. Trust me when I say you could do far worse in this castle."

"But—" I began.

"I have made my decision," he said.

"Mar Mar has made his decision," the fembots repeated.

He gave a dismissive wave and headed back to his dark throne.

CHAPTER 30

THE WALL WALK
OF DOOM

MISHDRONE GRABBED ME forcefully by the arm and led me from the throne room. Four fembots fell in line behind us.

I trudged down the dark stones of the cavernous castle hallway, not sure what level of sadness to settle on. Surviving a direct encounter with Mar Mar and getting my bounty lowered was a definite victory. Plus, getting Forglyn thrown into the dungeon was a major upswing of justice. But, for all that, I was getting marched off to a jail cell.

As Mishdrone's strong, metal fingers dug into my arm, I thought about what a bittersweet moment this was.

We rounded a corner and I heard a soft thud behind us. I looked back and three fembots were following us. Their glowing white eyes were scanning the area as if looking for something. I could've sworn there were four of them when we left the throne room.

Mishdrone urged me forward, leading our procession up a steep ramp. Another soft thud sounded behind us. Only two fembots followed now. Their swords were at the ready as they swiveled from side to side as if waiting for an attack.

There were only two possibilities. Either some hideous creature had escaped the dark dungeons and was taking us out one by one or someone was coming to my rescue. Although the former was far more likely, I held great hope for the latter.

We ascended from the lower hallways onto the castle walls. Twin moons and distant stars shone down on us, illuminating the vast and well-fortified dark castle. An unending array of huge, black stones and thick steel reinforcements stretched out before us.

I glanced back and saw the blur of a stealthy, black-suited figure swing across the wall walk and take out the remaining two fembots. As the figure disappeared over the battlements, I caught a glimpse of silver and electric blue hair. The owner, of course, was quite possibly the greatest woman that ever lived. My spirit soared.

I was alone with Mishdrone. His iron grip on my arm and his steady trudge forward were the marks of someone dead set on a mission. He was so focused on the task at hand, he was oblivious to the loss of his fembot escort.

Obviously, Mishdrone wouldn't rest until he saw me locked up in prison. No doubt he also had a few thoughts about roughing me up a bit first. Leaving me with no option but to blast him into small, metal bits.

"So, Mishdrone," I spoke casually. "You probably don't want to hang onto my weapon too long. Remember what happened last time?" I made a theatrical exploding sound.

Mishdrone stopped and spun me around. The wide band on his head glowed a bright red. A metal panel in his side opened and out slid my DEMOTER X. He took the weapon in his hand and pointed over the castle walls. He leaned back, preparing to throw the pistol in the same direction.

Jasette sprang over the battlements, arcing toward us, a strand of energy string contracting in her hand. Her other hand held one of her trademark silver blasters, aimed directly at Mishdrone.

Red energy blasts spun the cyborg sideways. My DEMOTER was knocked free from his hand and went clattering across the stone floor. I dove for it, retrieving the weapon and rolling to face Mishdrone in the same fluid motion.

The cyborg let out a cry like the rending of metal and reached down for me. I squeezed off three blasts in rapid succession. With a bright flash of white and a metallic screech, Mishdrone careened backward over the battlements.

I lay there, frozen for a moment, catching my breath and reveling in the glorious scene that just took place.

Jasette ran over to me. "Glint, get up. We have to go."

A wave of relief washed over me. I stood quickly. "Jasette, you're okay." I grabbed her and gave her a strong kiss.

She pulled back, a smile on her face. "As much as I like that, there's no time." Her fingers danced out quick commands on her forearm computer.

"I thought you'd been captured?" I said.

"I was. All of us were, before Blix freed us. Apparently he'd rigged our bracelets early on in case things got ugly and we needed to escape. When we couldn't find you and saw Forglyn leaving Glittronium in a rush, we knew he'd taken you." She gave a curious glance at my shoulders. "What happened to your wings? And your hands?"

"Glittronium plastic surgery."

She gave a bemused look. A tone sounded on her computer, followed by Nelvan's voice. "Jasette?"

"Yes, Nelvan, I got him. Start the sequence."

"Okay."

Jasette turned to me and smiled. "I have to say, I'm thoroughly impressed. I can't believe you won."

"That makes two of us."

"Um," Nelvan's voice sounded unsure. "So, it's blue, then red, then down three-fourths on the light dial, right?"

"No, no, you have it reversed."

My stomach sank. "You're trusting Nelvan with a teleport?"

"I gave him a crash course; he'll be fine." Jasette looked far from confident. "Okay, Nelvan. Let's start with—" A metal cable wrapped around Jasette's neck and cut her words short. She let out a choking sound as the cable pulled her backward.

Horror washed over me at the sight of Mishdrone clinging to the edge of the battlements. He gripped the dark stone with one hand and pulled Jasette toward him with the other.

I rushed to Jasette, struggling to remove the steel cable from her neck. The metal wouldn't budge. A tinge of regret went through me at the loss of my strong lizard hands.

"Jasette, you cut out," Nelvan's voice sounded from her forearm computer. "You said to turn the light dial down three-fourths first, right?"

Jasette's tried to speak, but her words were cut short. Her face turned red as she nodded and motioned toward her computer.

"Yes, Nelvan," I shouted. "The light dial first."

"Got it," he said.

Jasette drew a silver blaster and fired blindly at the cable behind her. Her blasts left sections of the cable darkened and pitted, but intact.

Another pull from Mishdrone sent us to the floor of the wall walk. I drew my pistol and aimed it at the filthy cyborg's head peeking over the stones. Jasette grabbed my arm and mouthed the word "no." She made an arcing motion with her hand. Her message was clear. If Mishdrone fell off the wall, he would take her down with him.

Dozens of fembots emerged on the castle walls. Apparently Jasette's dispatching of our fembot escort and our scuffle on the wall walk hadn't gone unnoticed.

The fembots charged toward us, their red laser swords held high, ready to attack.

I switched my target to the cable and fired away. A series of metallic screeches sounded as the energy blasts found their mark. Several twisted metal shards broke away from the cable, leaving it far thinner. The cable was badly damaged but still functional.

Mishdrone gave another pull on the cable, bringing Jasette within his reach.

"No!" I cried out as I ran to her. I grabbed her at the same moment Mishdrone put both hands on the cable and pulled her over the wall. My feet lifted off the ground, and the three of us careened over the battlements. At that moment, I really missed my wings.

CHAPTER 31

TELEPORTATION SLEIGHT OF HAND

FALLING HEADFIRST down a towering castle wall is enough to wipe any logic or strategy out of your head and leave you with nothing but sheer terror. But seeing the desperate face of Jasette before me, plunging to her doom, set my mind to action.

I still had an iron grip on the DEMOTER. I trained it on the damaged section of cable—which wasn't easy while in freefall—and let fly a hurricane of energy blasts.

Somewhere around the seventh blast I heard a loud snap and an eerie cry from Mishdrone.

"Jasette? Captain?" Nelvan's voice sounded from the forearm computer. "I activated the light dial. Now I hit the blue control and then the red one, right?"

My eyes widened at the sight of the ground rushing toward us. "Yes. Hurry!"

"No," Jasette choked out. "Red! Then blue!"

"Okay, here goes," Nelvan said.

I closed my eyes and prepared for impact.

A bright beam of light surrounded us. The ground, the castle, and the filthy cyborg disappeared in a flash of light.

A freem later we collapsed on the floor of the transport room on Forglyn's space cruiser. Nelvan was manning a holoscreen control panel nearby. The floor was littered with fallen security guards.

Nelvan threw his arms up and let out a victory shout. "Yes! It worked!"

I helped Jasette to her feet and pulled the severed section of cable from her neck. It dropped to the ground with a loud clanking sound.

"Good job, Nelvan." Jasette coughed while rubbing her reddened neck.

I held her close. "You all right?"

She nodded. "Fine. Let's never do that again, okay?"

"Deal." I looked at the fallen guards on the floor. "Looks like you left your mark here already."

She chuckled. "Nothing a few concussion discs couldn't handle."

A thunderous impact rocked the ship.

She grabbed me by the arm. "Come on, we're not out of this yet." She led me over to Nelvan and went back to the controls on her forearm computer. "We have to hurry before they blow us to pieces."

"Who?" I said.

"Mar Mar's ground defenses," she said. "Any unauthorized teleportations result in termination. Standard thug lair procedure."

She tapped a few buttons on her computer before grabbing Nelvan's hand so we were all linked together. "Blix, you have us?"

Blix's voice came through her computer. "Excellent work Jasette, I must say—"

"No time!"

"Quite right," Blix said. "Hold very still. Our dusty teleporter is still acting up."

Jasette grimaced. "I'm still nauseous from the last trip."

I turned to her in horror. "You brought my teleporter back online?"

She shot me a look of death. "If you'd kept that thing in running order, it wouldn't be such a risky venture now that we're forced to use it."

A loud crack sounded in Forglyn's ship. The structure trembled and creaked. Several pressure cracks formed on the walls.

"Hurry, Blix!" Jasette said.

A sluggish orange energy swirled around our feet, making its way up our legs. The ship swayed and the cracks spread down the walls at a far greater speed than the swirling energy moved over us.

"Can't this thing go any faster?" I said.

"Captain," Blix said. "We haven't used the teleporter in over three gloons. We're lucky it's even functioning. In fact, Nelvan, make sure to—"

"Trust me, I'm praying," Nelvan said.

The orange energy swirled around our heads now. Large sections of wall broke loose and streams of fire burst forth. Jasette tightened her grip on my hand.

My stomach churned, and I had the unnerving feeling my body was being flattened. "This doesn't feel right," I said.

Jasette squeezed my hand harder. This time it felt more like she was trying to hurt me rather than gaining comfort. I felt myself go weightless just as the walls around us exploded into flying shrapnel and fireballs.

A freem later we appeared in the transporter room on my ship. The room was filled with old storage containers and broken parts strewn about the floor. Ever since I took the transporter offline three gloons ago, due to the fact that teleportation was pure evil, it had basically served as a storage room.

My head felt dizzy from the teleport. A few unholy rumblings from my stomach sent predictions that vomit could be in my future.

Blix was manning the control panel nearby. "Iris, they're back. Get us out of here using my precise coordinates."

"Welcome back, Glint," Iris said. "I'm glad you're safe. I mean, I'm glad everyone's safe."

I gave a wary look at the ceiling. I made a mental note to comb the uniweb for tips on disenchanting overly friendly ship computers. The ship lurched and I felt the sensation of speed.

Jasette collapsed on the floor, breathing a sigh of relief. "Great job, guys. I can't believe we made it."

"Don't be too hasty." Blix was focused on the control panel, his fingers tapping out quick commands. "We were far from Forglyn's ship, but Mar Mar's sensors are powerful. If my calculations were correct, the explosion should help mask our teleportation sleight of hand but there's a slight chance that—"

A long beep sounded. Blix froze. "I'm getting something. Lots of moving objects. Could be Mar Mar's star fighter fleet." Blix gave a worried look toward us. "Ouch."

I hurried over to the control panel. Dozens of small red

dots were moving across the screen. "What class of fighter? Can we outrun them?"

"Doubtful." Blix tapped out a few more commands. "Wait." Blix enlarged a section of the screen. "False alarm." He learned back and chuckled. "Just a meteor shower. We're clear."

Even though I knew it would cause him little or no pain, I gave Blix a solid punch on his scaly shoulder. "Thanks for scaring me to death."

Blix looked at his shoulder and grinned. "Is that the best you can do?"

Nelvan met us at the control panel, scanning it as if to make sure. "So, that's it? We're safe?"

"We're still in long-range danger," Blix said. "We should head to the bridge for more thorough scans."

"Yeah," I said. "By the way, how'd you manage to escape Forglyn?"

Blix straightened his dagger straps. "'A Vythian bereft of preemptive attacks is a Vythian destined to peril.'"

"I have no idea what that means," I said.

Blix frowned. "A high stakes competition like the Iron Gauntlet is sure to have its share of underhanded assaults. Sure enough, when Forglyn wanted to fit us all with those competitor's bracelets, I knew that would be our first undoing. That's why I grabbed them all before they went on our wrists and put disruptors on the inner surface. It allowed me to free us once I was reunited with the others."

Nelvan smiled and patted Blix on the back.

"Rule number one about visiting potentially hostile planets ..." Blix lifted his finger in the air as if accenting an important point to a classroom. "If they want to put something on your wrist, ankle, or neck, you'd better presume it will turn into shackles should things go awry."

"I'm just glad Glint made it out of that throne room alive." Jasette joined us at the control panel. "When I couldn't get past the inner security, I thought the game was up. Then there you were, walking down the outer hallways with only a cyborg and four fembots." Jasette shifted her body into a confident pose. "Please, give me a real challenge."

"That was fortunate, indeed." Blix turned to me, an inquisitive look on his face. "I'm curious to learn how you survived a direct encounter with Mar Mar the Unthinkable."

I pulled my jacket tight and gave a confident grin. "Okay, but get ready to be impressed with your captain."

CHAPTER 32

THE GHOST SHIP

AS WE HEADED BACK to the bridge, I filled my crew in on the Silvet–Selinxia shape changer and the false wager. Somehow my brave efforts in keeping it a secret to protect them didn't go over as well as I'd hoped. Blix said something about all crewmembers needing to be present for any deal putting the crew at risk. Even after I remembered the vibe bar in my jacket pocket and the vibe spheres tucked away in my chambers, they weren't happy with my decision.

It was a losing battle, so I switched the story to my encounter with Mar Mar. It was beautiful recounting how I outwitted Forglyn and sent him crying to the dungeons and wailing about how much smarter and better looking I was. At least, that's how it happened in my retelling.

Once I got started, I found it incredibly easy to embellish the story in my favor. This had the unfortunate side effect of putting my entire story in question with my crew. After several moments of threats and begging, they agreed to accept the basics of what happened: I'd escaped Mar Mar's throne room, tricked him into taking the Emerald Enigma, and Forglyn was sent to the dungeons. The only thing still hanging in doubt was Mishdrone.

Try as I might, they refused to believe the creepy cyborg was a twisted amalgam of Hamilton Von Drone and Mishmash. However I pleaded my case, they couldn't seem to accept that reality. Even Jasette, who'd almost plunged to her death at his hand, doubted my story. Blix said my "tale of Mishdrone," as he called it, was my overblown sense of "nemesis bitterness." He claimed it was influencing my "perception of reality." He kept using finger quotes to accent his psychobabble until I was tired of arguing.

I gave up trying to persuade the crew, since it would only lead to more long-winded psychoanalysis by Blix. I'd just been through a harrowing adventure, and all I wanted to do was rest and take a vacation.

When we finally ended up back on the bridge of my ship, I felt like I was home.

"Systems at 86 percent, Captain." Blix called over his shoulder from the engineering station. "Quite positive considering the recent strain from the ill-functioning teleporter."

I nodded in hearty agreement. I was just happy to be free and flying again. The viewing screen displayed an endless array of stars before us.

I took a deep, relaxing breath. "The universe is ours. It's time we claimed some of it for our own. Who else is tired of being broke?"

Blix raised his hand.

"Several of my systems could use upgrading," Iris emitted a series of discordant bleeps as if to reinforce her point. "The vibes gained from a prosperous job could improve my overall performance and sense of well being."

"I've got about twenty thousand vibes," I patted the vibe bar in my jacket. "That's a good start."

"Well, it's not a million, but it's not bad, Glint," Jasette said.

It was a backhanded compliment, but a compliment nonetheless.

Jasette spun around to face me from the navigator's chair. "We're in a pretty remote system; we should probably head toward civilization. There's a small spaceport about a day's travel from here. You can probably find a piloting job there." Her face tightened. "Of course, I'll have to set off on my own once we arrive."

"What?" Nelvan said.

She gave him a sad smile. "Forglyn knew of the chrysolenthium flower. He knew my planet is vulnerable. My people have tried to keep it a secret but if he knew, others know as well." She turned back to me. "I've run out of time. I can't take another moment away from the search for that flower."

Nelvan gave a pleading look my way.

In the excitement of surviving the Iron Gauntlet, escaping Mar Mar, and being a free space captain with a myriad of piloting opportunities at my fingertips, I'd forgotten about the plight of Jasette's planet.

I couldn't argue with her logic about Forglyn's discovery. If he knew, there was a good chance other powerful people knew. Her planet was definitely a target for takeover.

She'd mentioned before that the Krennis sector was her best shot at finding the flower. From what I knew of it, most of the civilized settlements were filled with meager outpost dwellers. Not exactly a hot spot for finding a good payday.

Jasette watched me with a somber expression. She knew

this was throwing me for a loop. In my hazy confusion, one thought became clear. As I looked into her green eyes, I knew I couldn't let her face her troubles alone.

I made a theatrical look toward Blix. "Speaking of treasure, I've heard tales of old gemstone mines located in the Krennis sector, near the planet Jelmontaire."

Blix gave a sly smile and turned to his controls. "Locking in coordinates now, Captain."

Jasette smiled and her eyes teared up. "I could kiss you right now."

"No argument here," I smiled. "Just tell me there's a big reward from your kingdom for finding this crazy flower."

She gave an apologetic look. "Well, actually the search for it has left our funds kind of—"

I held my hands up. "Stop. Don't tell me. I'm just going to pretend there's a big reward."

She shrugged. "I suppose there's always a chance."

"Um … Captain?" Blix said.

"What?" I turned to Blix, irritated at being drawn away from Jasette's beautiful face.

His eyes were focused on the engineering screen. "We've got long-range energy beams, heading our way. Mar Mar's defenses were stronger than I'd hoped."

All my muscles tensed. We weren't free yet. "Put it on screen."

The visuals flickered to life, showcasing several bright orange beams streaming toward us like fiery comets.

"Level twelve quadrant seekers." Jasette sounded like the wind had been knocked out of her. "Move this thing quick."

"Blix." I turned to him. "Shields up. Evasive maneuvers."

His fingers flew across the controls. "Okay, but—oh, boy. Prepare for impact."

I gripped the armrests as a jolting blast rocked the ship. The lights flickered.

"Oh, Captain," Iris pleaded. "That was terrible. Help me."

Several more thunderous impacts hit the ship. A groan of stressed metal filled the bridge, and the lights went out. Emergency blue floor runners lit up.

"Captain," Blix said. "One more shot will—"

Another violent jolt hit the ship, and several systems powered down. The ship went into a slow roll.

"Iris," I said. "Full power. We need to get out of here."

"Glint," Iris spoke in a feeble voice. "Is that you? You sound so far away."

"We're in trouble. We need power."

"Where am I?" Iris said. "I can't feel my legs."

"We're on reserves, Captain." Blix turned toward me, a resigned look on his face. "Shields down and thrusters offline. I'm afraid we're at the mercy of space."

"Can we get visuals?" I said.

Blix nodded and hit a few controls. The visuals flicked on with a desolate view of stars.

"At least we didn't explode," Jasette said. "One more solid hit would've been the end of us."

"What's that?" Nelvan was squinting at the visuals.

I focused my attention forward. It took a moment to understand what I was seeing. It was as if the darkness between the stars was moving.

"It's an asteroid," Jasette said.

"No," Blix worked at the engineering controls. "I'm getting energy readings. Electronic emitters. It could be a ship."

"It's too big for a ship," Jasette said.

Blix studied the controls. "Yes. Perhaps it's a small space station adrift. Whatever it is, we're heading right for it."

The dark shadow grew and filled the screen. Small points of light blinked sparingly across its surface. It was clear it was a spacecraft, but much larger than I'd ever witnessed.

"I've never seen a ship like that," Jasette said.

I nodded in agreement. The cascading curves of the hull looked like something that was grown out of some giant alien's garden.

"The product of an ancient race, no doubt," Blix said. "Just a moment … I'm detecting a signal, Captain."

"A message?" I said.

"Hard to be sure. It's not translating exactly, but it could be a distress call."

Jasette turned to me, a questioning look on her face. "Sounds like a trap."

Space bar tales of a mysterious "ghost ship" flooded back to me. Memories of drunken star pilots leaning close with bloodshot eyes, whispering visions of a massive, dark ship that spelled certain doom for any space traveler unlucky enough to come across it.

A dim light shone out from the ship and connected with us.

"Ahh," Iris spoke as though in a dream. "That's nice, Captain. Very relaxing."

"Tractor beam," Blix said. "It's weak but it's enough to pull us in."

"What do they want?" Nelvan's voice trembled. "Are they dangerous?"

The dark ship moved closer, the soft light of the tractor beam making it look ghostly. A sense of dread crept over me. I swallowed hard, wondering how many of the legends were true.

ACKNOWLEDGMENTS

I am so thankful to family and friends for their support of my writing and for geeking out with me on science fiction. All my love to Jolene, Joshua, and Katie.

Thank you to Steve Laube and the talented staff at Enclave and Gilead Publishing. Also, thanks to Mark Gottlieb and Trident Media Group for continuing to believe in Space Drifters.

Huge credit goes out to those that took this book up several notches—Andy Meisenheimer for his editing expertise and Kirk DouPonce for an outstanding cover that breathed life into my characters.

Lastly, a shout out to the Writers Without Borders crew: Merrie Destefano, Rebecca LuElla Miller, Rachel Marks, and Mike Duran for their priceless feedback on my writing.